Thorough...
The sta...

Scandal has hit the...
award-winning Quest Stables. Find out what it will take to
return this horse-racing dynasty to the winner's circle!

Available July 2008

#1 *Flirting with Trouble* by Elizabeth Bevarly
Publicist Marnie Roberts has just been handed a PR disaster,
one that will bring her face-to-face with the man who walked
out of her bed and out of her life eight years ago.

#2 *Biding Her Time* by Wendy Warren
Somehow, Audrey Griffin's motto of "seize the day" has
unexpectedly thrown her into the arms of a straitlaced Aussie
who doesn't do no-strings-attached. Is Audrey balking at
commitment…or simply biding her time?

#3 *Picture of Perfection* by Kristin Gabriel
When Carter Phillips sees an exquisite painting that could be
the key to saving his career, he goes after the artist. Will he
sacrifice his professional future for a personal one with her?

#4 *Something to Talk About* by Joanne Rock
Widowed single mom Amanda Emory is on the run from her
past, but when she meets Quest's trainer she suddenly wants to
risk it all…and give everyone something to talk about!

Dear Reader,

I grew up just south of Saratoga Springs, New York, site of one of the prettiest racetracks in the country. As a teen, I often worked as a model during "Breakfast at the Track," tooling around from table to table to tell breakfast patrons in the grandstand's clubhouse about designer outfits. During that time, I had the pleasure to meet many people from around the country who came to summer in Saratoga for the August racing season. I met jockeys and trainers, horse owners, socialites and die-hard racing fans, all of whom fascinated this farmer's daughter who grew up on the banks of the Hudson.

So I couldn't wait to re-create that world for readers in *Something to Talk About.* Set on a Kentucky horse farm and rooted in the small racing community that transports itself to Saratoga every year, this book has been a pure pleasure to write, evoking lots of fun memories for me. I hope you enjoy the thrill, the beauty and the power of the Thoroughbreds, and, most of all, I hope you enjoy the passion of the people behind them.

Happy reading!

Joanne Rock

Thoroughbred Legacy

SOMETHING TO TALK ABOUT

Joanne Rock

Silhouette Books

Published by Silhouette Books
America's Publisher of Contemporary Romance

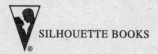

SILHOUETTE BOOKS

ISBN-13: 978-0-373-19917-4
ISBN-10:   0-373-19917-1

SOMETHING TO TALK ABOUT

Special thanks and acknowledgment are given to Joanne Rock
for her contribution to the Thoroughbred Legacy series.

Visit Silhouette Special Edition and Thoroughbred Legacy
at www.eHarlequin.com.

Printed in U.S.A.

JOANNE ROCK

is a three-time RITA® Award nominee who didn't think to indulge her love of writing when she went to college, instead opting for a communications degree and a business minor involving far too much accounting. Only after venturing into the real world did she realize it would have been wiser to study what she liked best so she could enjoy her life's work. Heading back to university for a graduate degree in English literature, Joanne penned her first novel while she was also writing her thesis. It took the rejection of six completed novels before she sold her first book, but she never regretted the career choice based on a labor of love. Today Joanne lives in the Adirondack region of upstate New York with her husband and three sons, and she is thrilled to pen contemporary and historical romances for Harlequin Books. Visit her Web sites, www.joannerock.com or www.myspace.com/joanne_rock to enter monthly contests and learn more about her work.

To my mom and dad
Thank you for allowing me to have so many
cool life experiences at a young age, without which I
wouldn't have half as much material for my stories!
In particular, for the sake of this story, thank you
for the rides to Saratoga, long before I had my license,
so I could be a part of the glittering horse-racing world
if only for a few hours at a time.

Many thanks to my friend from the Bluegrass State,
Jan Scarbrough, who provided me extra insights on
Thoroughbred racing and horses in general. Any errors
in regard to my horse-trainer hero are strictly my own.

Chapter One

"But you'd really like this guy. Honest."

Amanda Emory had grown accustomed to fending off suggestions on her love life from girlfriends and her well-meaning mother. But listening to dating advice from her nine-year-old son seriously pushed the limit.

"Kiefer, I'm sure he's a very nice man." Distracted by the sight of the movers carrying her sons' bunk beds up the stairs of the small condo unit they'd purchased, Amanda called instructions for placing the furniture she'd picked out with her husband mere days before he died. And damn it, didn't those memories still catch her when she least expected them?

"He's not just nice, Mom." Kiefer stole a granola bar out of his younger brother's hand as he settled himself at the island separating the light-filled kitchen and a living room overrun with boxes. "He trains the horses and he can ride like the guys in cowboy movies. He knows everything about horses. Seriously, Mom. Everything."

Amanda retrieved a new granola bar for Max, her six-year-old, who had already found friends in the condo next door and was happily showing the other kids his latest creation with a building set among the piles of boxes. Amanda gave Max two extra treats for his friends and then tried to focus on Kiefer's latest matchmaking effort.

Although Dan had been dead two years, Kiefer's quest to see his mother remarried hadn't started until about three months ago, after he'd seen some movie about kid spies who—in the subplot—tricked their widowed parents into meeting and falling in love. In short order, Amanda had been steered toward Kiefer's soccer coach, the librarian at his school, a neighbor in their building back in Los Angeles, and now this…a horse trainer?

"He works with horses?" She settled into the seat next to him at the counter and swallowed back a pinch of motherly guilt that they hadn't spent much time together in the mayhem of moving halfway across the country to Woodford County, Kentucky. She'd had so much more on her mind than she could ever burden her boys with, but not for the world would she want them to feel they were anything but her top priority.

For now, she waved the deliverymen upstairs to settle the dresser wherever they wanted.

"He's the best. I watched him working with one of the colts while you were setting up your new office Friday." Kiefer scrubbed a finger over a gold fleck in the granite countertop, his dark-brown hair falling sideways over one eye like his father's. This summer, her oldest son seemed to be all arms and legs, his body growing faster than his meals could fill it out. "I'm going back tomorrow after school."

"Are there other kids who watch the horses then?" She hoped Kiefer would make friends in their new hometown. Having lived in suburban L.A. all her life, she was a little intimidated about uprooting her family to move to a community that was both rural and—to a large extent—wealthy. She'd chosen a neighborhood in Twisted River, removed from the immediate domain of Quest Stables, which was both her new employer and a megamillion-dollar business.

Kiefer shrugged.

"I don't know. But it doesn't matter." He peered up at her with the earnest eyes of a child who hadn't quite mastered the preteen ability to mask his feelings. "I don't like the other kids here anyway and I'm helping you…you know. Meet people."

Amanda's heart squeezed tight that her firstborn had been put in a position where he felt that he needed to take care of her. He sounded years older than he was, even if the scrapes on his elbows and the jelly stain on his shirt gave him away as the kid he deserved to be.

"I appreciate you, baby." She hugged him tight, grateful that he still let her. "And I think it's great that you want to look out for me, but I promise you when the time is right, I'll think about socializing."

That much was true. And she didn't have the heart to share her fear that the opportunity might not come for a very long while. She didn't know why no one had turned her head in the two years since her police sergeant husband had been gunned down in a drug bust, but the grief counselor from the LAPD had assured her that it was okay to mourn on her own timetable and that healing would come when her heart dictated.

Kiefer looked ready to argue, his brow knitted in concentration as if he were reaching for the right words, when Max and his new pals came barreling over. They each waved some kind of airplane they'd made with Max's new construction set, although the little girl's plane looked more like a flying bunny rabbit.

While Amanda doled out praise for all the creations, Kiefer somehow disappeared. The movers shouted for a clear path into the dining room as they wheeled in a small hutch on a dolly.

Kiefer's matchmaking would have to wait, although his penchant to fix her up wasn't nearly as troublesome to her as his lack of effort to meet kids his own age. But since she wasn't exactly the Mingle Queen herself, how could she blame him?

The phone on the kitchen wall rang as the kids flew their toys into the laundry room. Amanda picked it up on the first ring, grateful her number was working. They'd been camping out in the condo for almost a week while waiting for the moving truck, but the phone company had somehow overlooked them until today.

"Hello?"

Silence answered her.

"Hello?" She swallowed down an old panic, knowing sometimes it took a moment for telemarketers to come on the line. She'd been scared by that phenomenon before.

But still no one answered. The silence mounted. Expanded. And then *click*. The line disconnected as the other party hung up.

In an instant, two years' worth of worry came flooding back. Her knees buckled. She'd moved halfway across the country to escape the possibility of revenge from a drug gang. Dan had killed one of the group's members before taking a fatal bullet himself, and the dead man's brother—Benny Orway—had promised revenge at his trial two years ago.

Amanda had uprooted her kids before the guy was released from prison a week ago, unwilling to take any chances with the kids' safety. But she'd started receiving late-night hang-up calls the month before she'd relocated. The calls spooked her, making her all the more grateful for the job offer in Kentucky.

As she hung up the phone, her hands shook just a little, even as she told herself hang-ups happened all the time.

"Mrs. Emory?" one of the movers shouted from the front hall, his arms full of garment bags that must have spilled out from one of the boxes.

"Coming." Willing her heart to quit racing, she put one foot in front of the other to address a crisis so much easier than the one she'd run two thousand miles to escape.

But as the silence of the phone call echoed in her ears, Amanda hoped she'd run far enough.

Normally, Robbie Preston didn't mind Mondays.

He liked hard work and he was devoted to making his family's business, Quest Stables, the best Thoroughbred facility in the country. And although his family thwarted his efforts half the time, this Monday their maneuvering ticked him off more than usual.

"Marcus is making the rounds, Robbie." His sister, Melanie, breezed into the stable office after her morning workout with Leopold's Legacy. The horse had been destined to be a Triple Crown Winner for Quest before a DNA test revealed the sire of record, Apollo's Ice, was not the biological sire, and Legacy had been banned from racing in North America.

At five feet tall, Melanie had turned her love of riding into a full-fledged profession as a jockey, a gig that ensured she had no competition from within the Preston clan.

Unlike him.

But since his sister was the only member of his immediate family to have even a small amount of respect for his skills as a trainer, Robbie tried to keep his cool when she brought up his least favorite topic.

"I hope no one expects me to lead the welcoming committee. I've managed to avoid him since our confirmation at Del Mar." He poured himself a cup of coffee from a pot someone had started long before dawn. The stables ran on an early schedule, and most of the animals were in the paddocks or on the exercise track by sunrise.

The new trainer had been in residence at Quest for the last few weeks, but Robbie had purposely found other things to do than ease the transition for the guy. They'd had a hard enough time working together at the Del Mar races. But he knew the time had come to officially accept Marcus, no matter how awkward the meeting might be.

"Please tell me you're not going to create an international incident." Melanie dropped into a chair across from the office's main reception area, which lately saw very little traffic outside of the stable staff. On days when prospective clients wandered through the stable area to check out Quest's boarding and training facilities, the coffee would have been a whole lot fresher than the brew Robbie choked down this morning. Although, in all fairness, it might have been his own bitterness he tasted more than any java.

"Who's creating an incident?" He stalked around the office to work off the edges of an anger he'd tried hard to stuff down this last month. "I'm here, aren't I? Putting in my hours for the greater good despite a slap in the face that couldn't have been more direct. I know it's not Marcus's fault he won the head trainer slot and I know he's damn good at the job."

He scuffed his toe across the hardwood floor covered by a few thick wool throw rugs. And although the office was attached to the stables, the room lacked any scent of horses since it was outfitted to impress visitors. A few framed photos of Quest's most famous equine residents lined the walls.

"I know that too, but you would have done as well or even better considering you're as obsessive about your work as you are about—oh—everything else you've ever tackled." Melanie slid her feet out of her riding boots and tucked them under her. "Remember when you decided to take up cliff-diving?"

"Whoa. Anybody ever tell you that you've got a knack for backhanded compliments?" Still, Robbie took some solace in his sister's opinion, since she knew horses as well as anyone, and her endorsement meant a lot, even if it was sandwiched between insults. "And for your information, three emergency-room visits in one summer builds character."

"I seem to remember Dad saying it built a thicker head." She flashed him an evil grin and socked him gently in the gut as he paced past her chair.

He paused long enough to pull her hair gently in a reflex gesture—a remnant of their days as kids that had long ago turned into a sign of affection.

"You know I'm twenty-eight and that's still what the old man sees?" He looked out the window onto the front paddock area, which was more for show than anything, the greens immaculate even if summer was quickly sliding into fall. "Even when I train a Derby winner like Leopold's Legacy, Dad fixates on the fact that I broke my nose twice in a season."

"I'm not touching that one."

Turning back to Melanie, he watched her tip her head back in her chair and study him with assessing eyes, her delicate size belying a nature every bit as fierce as his.

"Neither am I." He looked back out the window in time to see Marcus Vasquez—a trainer who had come to Quest from Australia's Lochlain Stables, run by Robbie's cousin—walking toward the offices with a woman Robbie had never seen before.

"What do you mean?" Melanie rose to join him at the window.

Robbie was surprised it took a bit of effort to tear his gaze away from the pretty woman talking to the new head trainer. Her short hair blew around her face, the dark locks sunkissed with lighter streaks. She wasn't necessarily beautiful, but something about her face fascinated him. Her easy laughter reminded him of all the ways his life had grown too uptight. Too frustrating.

"I mean I'm not sticking around for another year of Preston dramas when this family is hanging on to financial security by its teeth."

He'd been angry about a lot of things in the past few months and it had all come to a head when his father had imported Marcus from halfway around the world even though Robbie had more than enough qualifications for the job. Considering Quest's reputation had been called into question when the Jockey Association withdrew Leopold Legacy's status as a Thoroughbred, given his uncertain paternity, the stables could have benefited from the cost-saving measures of hiring a family member.

"Please don't make any hasty decisions—"

Impatience fired through him and he found himself concentrating on the pretty brunette's smile to ease the rush of anger.

"This isn't hasty. I've had plenty of time to think it over and I've come to the conclusion that I'd rather not sit at the dinner table with people who don't respect what I do. I'll continue my training duties, but I'm going to get a place in town."

"You know what that will do to Granddad?" Melanie lowered her voice as Marcus approached the door to the small office and the mystery woman turned in another direction.

Who was she? The question was far more pleasant than the one about what his disappearance from the house would do to their eighty-six-year-old grandfather, Hugh Preston. The patriarch of the clan wasn't always in residence since he liked to indulge his passion for racing by touring the nation's tracks and betting on new horses with a few of his cronies. But when he settled back into life at Quest Stables, he always made it a point to seek out Robbie and share stories from his days as a young immigrant fresh off the boat from County Clare, Ireland.

His tales of hard work had inspired Robbie his whole life. And instead of looking at Robbie's hot-headed nature as a defect, Granddad liked to say Robbie simply had inherited the passionate nature of the Irish. The old man's words had often been a balm during his teenage years when Robbie and his father had been at odds more times than he could count.

"You don't fight fair," he complained, wondering how Melanie could have zeroed in so easily on Robbie's only reservation about moving off the Quest compound.

"With all the stress this family is under lately— especially Granddad at his age—I can't afford to fight fair."

Robbie would have liked to argue that Granddad wasn't growing frail of heart just because the rest of him was aging, but the door to the office opened.

Steeling himself to be civil, Robbie came face to face with the man who'd stolen his future out from under him.

Marcus Vasquez had been raised in Spain and his dark hair and eyes reflected the heritage. He had a reputation as a hardworking, practical man. Even Robbie's grandfather respected him, so at least Marcus had that much in his favor.

"Marcus." Robbie thrust out his hand and willed himself not to give in to a primitive urge to crush the guy's fingers. "Good to have you at Quest."

"Thank you." Marcus shook his hand easily, making direct eye contact before he nodded to Melanie. "I've enjoyed finding my way around here."

Instead of being back in Australia running Lochlain Stables where he damn well belonged. When Quest's previous head trainer, Daniel Whittleson, had left the job to work at Lochlain, he had recommended Marcus as his replacement. Robbie knew that—at thirty-two years old—Marcus wouldn't be vacating the Quest head trainer position anytime soon.

"I hope you'll let me know if I can help you with anything. Daniel left during a difficult time, considering the uproar around Leopold's Legacy." Until the mystery of Leopold's Legacy's parentage was solved, the horse had had to be withdrawn from racing and Quest's reputation teetered on the verge of ruin.

Hell, their financial stability teetered on the verge of ruin right along with it since their reputation had attracted the owners who paid big fees to have their horses stabled and trained here.

"Daniel and I have spoken extensively." Marcus's eyes veered briefly to Melanie's sock-clad feet. "I think I have things well in hand by now, but I appreciate the offer."

Beside him, Robbie sensed his sister straighten. Tense.

Hell, she couldn't be any tenser than him. Was Marcus implying he didn't need help running the training operation?

"Some of the trainers might have ideas about what

approach to take next." Diplomatically, he did not mention his own opinions. "Now that Legacy is out of racing—"

"There is no reason to believe Legacy is done. The horse was on the verge of a Triple Crown win."

A muscle kinked in Robbie's shoulders.

"But if he's not allowed to race again, shouldn't we have a plan for developing the *next* Triple Crown winner?" There was so much potential in the stables at Quest, but the most time and money was spent on a handful of top prospects.

"I would think we are always planning for that." Marcus gave a stiff nod to both of them. "Right now, we're lucky to be racing any horses at all. My priority is keeping all of our horses in top condition until this scandal with Legacy is cleared up."

With that, he left the office, stalking off to the stable or paddocks or wherever he was needed. Robbie's blood simmered at the guy's casual attitude about plans for the future.

"This guy is the salvation of Quest's future?" he asked himself as much as Melanie.

She slid back into her boots and said nothing for a long moment.

"He's done well since he's been here. We just need to give him a chance." She finally said the polite thing, but Robbie could tell her heart wasn't in it.

He left the stable office in a black mood, determined to get the hell out of Dodge today. He might not relocate all the way into Twisted River in deference to his grandfather, but he could at least move his things into one of the cabins where the other trainers lived.

That was all he was around here, anyway. Marcus's arrival had proven Robbie wasn't a Preston on the fast track to success in the family business. He'd always stood a little outside the family, so he might as well live that reality now. If not for his devotion to the horses he'd raised himself, and a passion for racing, he would have left long ago. And really, if not for his grandfather, Robbie might have been tempted to take a few of his horses and start up a small stable of his own.

It was still something to consider.

And he would. Right after he went into town to lift a toast to his displaced status. A day like this one surely deserved a drink.

Chapter Two

The next morning, Robbie remembered why he shouldn't drink.

He'd had a hell of a time drowning his anger until all hours, but since he didn't cut himself any slack on his workday, he'd rolled out of bed with a hangover to face the same problems he'd left the day before.

Now, he finished exercising one of the colts Daniel Whittleson had purchased for the stables and passed off the reins to a groom. The horse was fast, his carriage solid, but the animal was peaking too fast.

"How many more are you going to take out?" a child's voice called to him.

Robbie turned to see a scrawny kid watching him

from the fence around the practice yard. His spiky dark hair was lighter at the tips, and the boy looked like a mini surfer dude with his tanned skin and board shorts. He wore flip-flops and a faded T-shirt under an open sweatshirt.

Robbie couldn't remember seeing him around before, although with Quest's extensive staff, there were certainly plenty of kids who lived on the property.

"Who wants to know?" Robbie strode closer to the fence, not minding a break. Besides, he'd served enough time standing at that fence all by himself in his youth to appreciate being the odd man out.

Hell, for that matter, welcome to his life today. He never had quite caught up to Brent and Andrew, his two older brothers, in the old man's eyes.

"Kiefer Emory." The boy straightened his skinny shoulders, though his feet remained planted on the lowest wooden rail. "I'm learning about horses. You sure ride a lot of 'em."

Robbie couldn't identify the accent, which didn't have the softened vowels of a Kentucky native.

"I'm a hands-on trainer, so I like to ride them to test their skills." He leaned against the fence and soaked up the September sun. His hungover eyes finally seemed to be recovering from the perpetual squint he'd had earlier in the day. "And I'm Robbie Preston, by the way. Nice to meet you."

Kiefer shook his hand with unexpected serious-ness, like a mini grown-up. When he didn't say any more, Robbie prodded him.

"I don't think I've seen you around here before. Do your parents work at Quest?"

"My mom started as the new office manager. We moved from Los Angeles last week."

That explained the surfer-dude clothes. And Robbie remembered his own mother mentioning a new hire for the position. She'd decided to take a chance on the woman from L.A. because she was a widow.

A damn young widow if this kid was anything to go by. The idea of the boy hanging out at the rail by himself bugged Robbie.

"Welcome to Kentucky. And if you want to learn about horses, you've come to the right place." He was about to invite the boy into the stables to see the horses close up when a flash of color caught his eye.

Looking up, he spotted the woman he'd seen speaking to Marcus yesterday. Only now, all traces of her easy laugh had disappeared. She charged toward them with determined steps, her jaw set and her lips compressed into a flat, disapproving line.

"Kiefer," she called the moment she got within hearing range and then hastened her pace. "You're supposed to be with Max at the after-school program here."

The boy turned, hopping off the fence rail as his mother reached them, her silky blouse and flowered skirt fluttering lightly in the breeze.

"But I told you I was coming here to watch the horses after I got off the bus. Remember?" Kiefer gestured toward the fence rail.

Or…toward Robbie?

"Ah." The woman seemed to notice him then, her sharp brown gaze taking him in with the careful perusal of a protective mother and not even an ounce of feminine interest.

His ego definitely would have smarted if not for his knowledge that she'd lost a husband. He had no idea how long ago that might have happened, but he couldn't imagine the pain of losing someone that close to you.

"Robbie Preston, ma'am." He held out a hand to her, strangely eager for her to take it.

He'd noticed her yesterday and remembered her after only a quick sighting. That was unusual for him. Not that he didn't attract his fair share of female attention. But he'd been so focused on work the last few years—so hell bent on winning family approval and the chance to head up Quest's training program—that he hadn't spent much time dating. His relationships had been low-key and often pursued by the ladies who wanted them.

For a woman to turn his head without even trying was a new experience. Especially a widow with a son. Hell, his hangover must have scrambled his brains.

"Amanda Emory." She took his hand as briefly as possible, her short pink nails barely registering before her hand was back at her side. "I'm the new office manager and I'm so sorry if my son has been pestering you."

She looped an arm around the boy as if to whisk him away from a big, bad dragon.

The thought gave him pause. Had she been listening to family gossip about his supposed hothead nature? The idea rankled.

"He's been no trouble at all. In fact, I was just—"

"It won't happen again, I promise." She backed away, her short, sharp heels sinking into the soft earth while her skirt billowed gently around her legs.

Damn it.

"Mrs. Emory—" The name didn't sit right on his tongue and it didn't stop her anyway. He raised his voice slightly. "Amanda."

That one stopped her. She looked up at him again as if seeing him for the first time. And whoa. His ego was a hell of a lot more pleased with this encounter.

But before he could ask her a damn thing, she shuttered those pretty dark eyes and seemed to shake her head *no*.

"Sorry," she said. "I need to return to the office since I hate to make a bad impression my first week on the job." She offered him a half smile, but he noticed she never relinquished her firm—protective—hold on her son.

"I just want you to know I'd like to show Kiefer the stables sometime. If he's interested in horses it's something he won't want to miss." He grinned at the kid, recognizing he carried more clout with the boy than the mom.

Kiefer perked up as though he'd gotten a present.

"Can I, Mom?"

"Not today, but thank you very much, Mr.

Preston." Her feet kept moving, out of range, out of the influence of the legendary Robbie Preston temper.

Damn it, she had to have heard rumors to have lit out of there so fast. He watched her walk away, the gentle sway of her hips beneath her fluttery skirt drawing his eye despite his foul mood. He needed to get back to his work and not let the encounter bother him though.

Because, no matter what Marcus said about always being on the lookout for the next big champion, Robbie wasn't leaving matters to chance. He'd ride every horse in the stables to see what kind of new talent was on the rise.

After all, horses were a damn sight easier to understand than women, and Robbie planned to stick to what he knew best.

Amanda remembered her meeting with the youngest Preston with a mixture of regret and embarrassment during her lunch hour the next day as she observed three of the stable's trainers work with their horses in the practice yard. From the safety of the office window, she could view one particular man without him knowing.

And heaven help her, she wanted to watch.

She didn't feel embarrassed about that because she wasn't ready to date. Or at least she hadn't thought she was. It had thrown her for a big-time loop the day before when her heart had started palpitating over a man so much younger than her.

How could forty-year-old hormones not have better judgment when they had finally decided to kick in after a two-year nap? She closed her eyes and remembered her husband's face—a face still so beloved, but, dear heaven, it had been achingly long since she'd touched him. Heard his voice beside her in bed at night.

She knew Dan would never have wanted her to be alone for the rest of her life, so it wasn't guilt she felt. Maybe it was more a matter of not wanting to give any spare time to a relationship when her kids deserved all that she—as a single parent—could possibly offer them. Besides, she couldn't believe she'd experienced such a sharp twinge of awareness for a younger man who also happened to be her employer's son.

Opening her eyes, she took one last look at Robbie Preston from two stories up. His athletic form was all too apparent in well-worn Levi's and a gray T-shirt with the stable name printed in black. From what she'd heard, his temperament had put him at odds with the family more than once. But as she watched his easy way with the gray horse he led into the practice yard now, Amanda saw a sensitivity that belied the rumors about him. Her grandmother had been raised on a farm in northern California, and Granny swore that horses and dogs could size up a person faster than anything on two legs.

"Aren't the horses beautiful?"

Amanda started at the feminine voice behind her

and turned to find Jenna Preston, Robbie's mother and the woman who'd hired her. Amanda's cheeks heated to be caught staring, but thankfully, it hadn't occurred to her kind employer that her attention had been fixed on one particular man among the horses. And for heaven's sake, she needed to get her mind back on her work.

"I am still in awe of how beautiful Kentucky is." That much was true. "The meadows and wildflowers—and the grass is so lush and green here. *Everything* is so green. And the Quest property is incredible with the acres of four rail fences and all the buildings painted to match."

Jenna smiled, her blue eyes warm with pleasure. "I'm passing that compliment straight to our head groundskeeper. He takes a lot of pride in the property and it certainly shows." Moving closer to the window, she frowned. "Have you met my youngest son yet?"

Apparently Robbie had only just come into her view. He was eye-to-eye with the gray horse as if they were having a meeting of minds. Amanda couldn't help a smile at the thought and she understood why Kiefer had been so intrigued by this man.

"Actually, we met yesterday. I've been taking a late lunch to check on my two boys at the after-school program here and found my older son quietly hero-worshipping Robbie while he worked with the horses. I had to shuttle Kiefer back to Claudia's house."

Jenna brushed a restless hand through her wavy auburn hair, her eyes fixed on Robbie.

"He's upset about us hiring an outsider as head trainer." She turned to cock a halfhearted grin at Amanda. "And I'm not telling you any family secrets with that one—all of Quest knows that his father skipped over the most likely candidate for the head trainer position. I just wanted to let you know in case he was…surly with you."

"Not at all." She couldn't explain the sudden surge of defensiveness she felt on Robbie's behalf, since she hardly knew him, but it bubbled up nevertheless. "He couldn't have been kinder to my son, even offering to show him the stables. If anything, I'm afraid I'll have a hard time keeping Kiefer out of Robbie's hair."

Jenna looked thoughtful.

"He's good with kids. Katie and Rhea—my son Brent's twin girls—both adore him. I'm sure Robbie would welcome the distraction of Kiefer's company these days, so I hope you won't think twice about taking him up on the offer for a guided stable tour from an expert."

Jenna patted her arm with a maternal reassurance that Amanda had seen her dole out to several of the employees during her short time at Quest. Robbie's mother had given Amanda a chance at this job when she had no experience, just some online computer courses and a fierce will to get out of L.A.

So why would she be so reluctant to take a chance on her own son as head trainer?

"Maybe I will." Amanda tightened her grip on the

papers in her arm. "I'd better be getting back to work if I'm going to finish up with the file reorganization this week."

And she *really* needed to walk away from the window where Robbie Preston inspired such unexpected feelings.

"I appreciate you undertaking such a big project right away. I knew our last manager had let things slide in those months he was looking for other work, but I didn't realize how much of a mess the files had become until after he left."

"I think we'll all be able to work more efficiently once I'm done." Truly, Amanda could never have functioned with the disorganization the previous administrator had left, so she was grateful when Jenna gave her the green light to overhaul nearly every facet of office procedure. The staff was small—only eight other people under Amanda's direct supervision—but the other employees had been around long enough that it would have been a headache to implement changes without Jenna's blessing.

"And by the way, Amanda, we're hosting a small dinner party at the main house on Friday for a handful of local Thoroughbred owners who are also friends. Why don't you join us for drinks if you have time? I think it would be nice for you to put some faces to the names you must be seeing over and over again in your paperwork. We do strive to keep the business feeling like family despite our size."

Warmed by the invitation, Amanda was reminded

all over again how fortunate she'd been to land here, far away from her personal demons on the West Coast.

"I'd be delighted, Mrs. Preston. Thank you."

"Call me Jenna and it's a date."

With a quick wave, she was off again, no doubt to lift someone else's spirits or assist around the office any way she could. Amanda admired her generous nature and wondered if her family knew how much she contributed to the business in her understated way.

Amanda had no intention of letting Jenna Preston down—not in the office and not at the dinner party. That meant focusing on her job and not speculating whether a certain horse trainer would be in attendance at the Preston house Friday night.

Amanda wasn't going to be happy.

Robbie knew by the end of the week that he'd be hearing from Kiefer Emory's uptight mother sooner or later about the time her son had been spending around the stables. Robbie hadn't mistaken the disapproval in her eyes when she'd hauled Kiefer away the last time, but the boy had made a point of stopping by after school every day until Robbie reminded him he should be heading to the care program run by one of the women who lived on the property.

Today was no exception.

"Is this horse your favorite?" Kiefer called to him from his usual spot at the rail of the practice yard, his school backpack at his feet, his toes now respectably covered in boots instead of flip flops.

"What makes you ask that?" Robbie eased up onto the colt he was working with. "I spend equal time with all of my horses."

At least, he had for the last few weeks while trying to get a feel for where each of the Thoroughbreds stood in their training.

"You look at this one different." Kiefer shrugged, apparently disinclined to pinpoint his reason any more than that. "I can just tell."

Robbie patted the colt's neck and steered him closer to the rail so Kiefer could do the same.

"This one is called Something to Talk About and I think he's the next hot prospect for Quest Stables."

Robbie had never possessed the strange kind of equine intuitiveness his sister Melanie seemed to have, but he knew enough about horses to feel the potential for power in this one. The gray colt showed hints of racing brilliance on the track and his temperament caught Robbie's eye. The colt didn't mingle with the other horses, preferring to keep his own counsel. And there was a spiritedness about him, a proud determination that Robbie recognized all too well.

"You mean he's going to be a racing champion?" Kiefer stroked the animal's nose.

Behind Kiefer, Robbie noticed his nieces, Katie and Rhea. The twins had been bending over an electronic game until one pointed out Robbie and Kiefer.

"Hey, California!" Katie called, handing the game to her sister. "Did you learn to ride yet?"

The two ran off before Kiefer could respond,

clearly smitten with the boy who must be about a year older than them. But to Robbie's surprise, Kiefer flushed and he looked worried.

"Robbie, can you teach me how to ride? All the kids at school know how and they think—" He shook his head and seemed to change his approach. "Well, they all learned to ride a long time ago and I don't want to be the loser who can't."

"Son, if you think those girls see you as a loser, then you're really missing the boat on understanding females." Hell, even from a hundred yards away Robbie could still see his nieces' matched heads turning around to look at the new kid on the block.

"It's not about them." Kiefer's face flushed even deeper and Robbie figured if Amanda didn't get riled about him hanging out with Kiefer this week, she'd definitely get mad when she found out Robbie had been sharing advice about women with a boy who hadn't reached the age of interest in girls yet.

"Is anybody giving you a hard time at school?" Robbie would gladly put aside whatever awkwardness there might be with Amanda if Kiefer needed help with some snot-nosed bully.

"No." Kiefer shook his head quickly and lightly twisted some of the horse's mane around his finger. "But it's tough being the new guy. I knew everyone at my last school. We surfed and skateboarded there. Here, everyone rides."

Robbie considered the request, knowing he couldn't do jack to teach the boy anything without his mother's blessing. But Kiefer didn't exaggerate. In Woodford County, the kids who didn't own horses knew five other people who did. Growing up in this area meant you loved horses and basketball. It seemed genetically programmed.

"Have you asked your mother about some lessons?"

"She said I should join the stable's riding club." Kiefer looked up from his fascination with the horse's mane. "But all the kids there already know how to ride."

"Ah." Robbie hated to wade into this any deeper, but then again, hadn't he lived his whole life by jumping into challenging situations with both feet? "You think it might help if I talked to her about some private lessons?"

Kiefer's face lit up so fast Robbie couldn't help but smile even though he might have put himself on the warpath with Amanda.

"Would you?"

"I can't promise how soon it will be, but I'll try to track her down."

"She has to go to the main house tonight," Kiefer offered, hopping down from the fence. "I'm going to get my homework done in case she says we can start tomorrow."

"Kief—"

The kid was honest-to-God already booking it up the path to his caregiver's cabin, his backpack jouncing up and down as he ran. He turned and waved from about fifty yards away, his feet never slowing.

"Thanks, Robbie!" he shouted.

Something to Talk About danced sideways underneath him, impatient to begin while Robbie tried to figure out what he'd gotten himself into.

No doubt about it, he'd have to stop by the main house after work tonight. Kiefer Emory's eyes had been too damn hopeful for Robbie to do anything but give it his best shot with Amanda. Kiefer didn't know that Robbie's least favorite place to hang out these days was the main house where his family congregated, united in their mistrust of him.

How fitting that prickly Amanda would be joining their ranks.

Since he'd moved out of the Preston family residence that week without a word to anyone, the evening promised to be interesting.

Chapter Three

Crap.

Robbie might have turned around before he got to the door of the main house if it hadn't been for his memory of Kiefer's face today. He knew what it was like to want to fit in so badly—a feeling he'd wrestled with where his brothers were concerned all his life. But he hadn't expected to show up at the house while his family was entertaining. The cars in the driveway could have been the showroom for a high-end dealership or the VIP parking lot at Saratoga or Keeneland. His parents' friends tended to be as wealthy as they were and could afford horses even more expensive than their cars—and that was saying something.

"Mister Robbie, we've been hoping you would

join us." Betsy Fuller, the Prestons' household manager, held the door of the sprawling redbrick house wide, her simple dress more that of a maid than of a woman earning the fat salary Robbie knew she collected for running a property bigger than some country clubs.

It was part of Betsy's charm that she'd never commented on family politics or Robbie's long absences. She had open arms and extra place settings for anyone who showed up on the doorstep and it was one of the many reasons everyone adored her.

"I didn't know they were entertaining tonight or I wouldn't have shown up in work clothes." Beyond Betsy, Robbie could see the candles lit throughout the downstairs, giving the place a festive look despite the heavy dark wood of the moldings and banisters, the rich burgundies and reds of the upholstered furniture. He knew all the guests would be out having cocktails on the veranda before dinner and he planned to make sure he avoided the family at all costs.

"If you hurry, you can change before they sit down." She checked her watch to make sure and then winked at him. "I can usually talk Judge Parker into an extra bourbon before dinner."

"Thanks, but I can't stay. I just came to speak to Amanda Emory if she's here." He stepped deeper into the front hall, peering around as if she might come into view any second. "Have you met the new office manager?"

"Of course I have." Betsy appeared mightily

offended at the idea that she would ever be unaware of family business. "She's out back with the family for cocktails, son. Now, why don't you go upstairs and get dressed?"

Robbie had left some clothes here when he'd moved out earlier in the week, so technically, he could make an appearance. But damn it, he wasn't going to play the family game of pretending he belonged here when they'd made it all too clear to him that he wasn't good enough to take on a big role at Quest.

"No thanks." He shook his head, regretting more than anything that he had to disappoint Betsy. She'd never treated him any differently than anyone else in the family. "Would you mind just letting her know that I'm here if I promise to have her back before you move into the dining room?"

If Betsy had an opinion on that, she kept it to herself, settling for a quick nod.

"I'll pass along the message."

She hurried off through the house while Robbie waited out front, the strains of a violin mingling with laughter from the veranda. His eyes went to the portraits of horses lining the walls. In other rooms, there were photographs and paintings of people. But here in the foyer there were horses dating back to Hugh Preston's earliest days at Aqueduct Racetrack in Queens where he'd first studied horses and made his earliest bets. There was a photo of Hugh with Clare's Quest, the little filly who'd brought his first big win.

Marching across the hunter-green walls were paintings of Old Barley, the stallion that had given Hugh a win at Saratoga to finance the family's move to Kentucky, followed by more horses that had all added to a family fortune spread across two continents. There weren't many portraits of horses from Robbie's cousins' farm in Hunter Valley, Australia, but there were a few. He looked at them now instead of thinking about Amanda Emory's potential reaction to his visit.

"Robbie?"

Her voice surprised him, even though he'd been expecting her.

He turned to find a far more sophisticated woman than he remembered. Her pretty dark hair and eyes were the same, but the outfit she wore… Damn it, he had no business taking in the soft curves of her slender frame, but the simple strapless blue cocktail dress she wore seemed to demand it. She'd thrown a yellow lace shawl around her shoulders, but it didn't hide much of anything. Another hint of lace peeked out below the dress's knee-length hem, accentuating her legs and drawing his gaze much too low.

Hell.

"Sorry to take you away from the group." He launched into conversation to recover from the awkward moment. "I won't keep you."

He waited for her to run away from him, as she had that day by the practice yard, or to come up with some excuse why she couldn't speak to him, since he supposed she'd been influenced by popular opinion regarding his character. Instead, she smiled warmly, the way he remembered from the first time he'd seen her.

"Actually, I'm really glad to see you."

He wondered if his eyes widened as much as he felt they did.

Probably they did, since she laughed.

"I mean it. And I'm sorry if I seemed short with you the day we met, but it's stressful starting a new job and I worried about taking time away to oversee Kiefer."

She smelled delicious—like flowers and maybe vanilla. He wanted to lean in for a more definitive sniff.

"He's a great kid." He wanted to make it clear that he didn't mind Kiefer's presence around the stables.

And he definitely wanted to remember why he was here since it didn't have anything to do with ogling a woman he had no business pursuing.

"Thank you." She smiled with maternal pleasure and managed to look even more beautiful than she had two minutes ago. "I'm very proud of both my boys but sometimes it's hard to step back from the day-in and day-out worries to appreciate how really great they are. I'm fortunate."

"You have two sons?" Robbie knew Kiefer hadn't mentioned a brother, but the boy had been fairly wrapped up in learning about horses all week.

"Max is six and Kiefer is nine. And actually, I've been meaning to seek you out to thank you for the time you've spent with Kiefer this week. He feels more sure of himself at school now that he can talk about horses without sounding like a total outsider."

"That's why I'm here." Robbie lowered his voice as one of the maids hurried through the foyer with a vase of flowers. No doubt they were trying to get the dining room prepped for the meal. The laughter of the cocktail crowd drifted through the halls.

"He's starting to get underfoot? I can—"

"No. Nothing like that." He put a hand on top of her fluttering one, a reflex reaction to her concern that suddenly drop-kicked him in the libido. The feel of her soft skin under his palm sent a surge of heat clean through him, the awareness a palpable thing between them.

She stilled, frozen, her hand in midair beneath his. He would have moved away faster if he could have sent the proper set of messages along his neurons, but his body didn't seem to obey. He stood there for a long moment, absorbing the silken texture of her and breathing her scent.

She recovered first, snatching her hand away quickly even if the reaction had been delayed.

"Then what is it?" Her words were a little breathless, or was that just wishful thinking on his part?

"Kiefer wants to learn how to ride." He was grateful for the words once he got them past his lips. They gave him something new to think about.

"I know he does, but honestly, I can't afford—"

"Amanda, you haven't gotten to know the

Prestons well enough yet if you think we would want you to pay for outside lessons when you work at the biggest horse-training facility in the Commonwealth of Kentucky."

"Really, I couldn't ask for any special favors." Her words were firm, her posture perfectly straight. She had "good girl" written on her so clearly he couldn't help but smile, although he didn't find her ethics half so amusing as he found his attraction to someone so sweetly upstanding. His sketchy track record with women ran more to the hell-raising variety, but there was no denying his physical response to Amanda.

"It's not a special favor." He gestured to the house behind her. "You're already standing in my mother's foyer, having cocktails with the neighbors. Trust me when I tell you, we want you to feel like family here." He might not agree with all the family's decisions, but Robbie was proud of the way they treated their staff. The corporate culture was decidedly down-home here. "And I just wanted your blessing that Kiefer has permission to ride before I let him on a horse. But I hope you'd never consider outsourcing riding lessons when you live here. We tend to know our horses around Quest Stables."

She grinned. "I guess you have a point there."

"As long as you don't mind, I can send Kiefer back to school with enough horse knowledge to set the other kids back a few steps." His knowledge might not impress the old man, but it could knock the socks off fourth graders.

"That would be really generous of you." She pulled the thin lace shawl tighter around her shoulders, clenching the fabric hard as if she could ward off the attraction zinging around the room. "But if he gets to be any trouble, I hope you'll let me know."

"I can do that. Although the traditional way to straighten out any troublemaking in a stable is to present the offender with a pitchfork and a stall for mucking."

"I see you know kids better than I realized."

"I've had a bit of a history with troublemaking myself."

"And your days with a pitchfork successfully reformed you?"

"I'm going to have to plead the Fifth on that one."

Behind Amanda, the voices from the veranda grew louder as two men disputed the racing odds at an upcoming meet. A door slammed and the violin stopped playing.

"They must be coming in for dinner." Amanda turned toward the sound before glancing back at him. "I'm not staying for the meal, but I should go in and make my goodbyes before they sit down."

He nodded, not wanting to cross paths with his family yet.

"Fine. I'll wait for you and walk you to your car." He didn't know why he offered.

No, he knew why he offered. He wished he had a little more restraint since she was clearly reluctant where he was concerned.

"That's not necessary. Thank you for the offer of lessons for Kiefer." She stepped away, eager to please his parents and play the proper guest.

"Not a problem." He smiled genially, but stood his ground and waited for her return.

She might think they had settled matters between them now that they'd agreed on Kiefer riding. But in Robbie's mind, they'd only succeeded in uncovering a bigger issue. And like any elephant in a room, the attraction between them wouldn't go away just because they ignored it.

These had to be some of the warmest people Amanda had ever met.

She shook hands with several of the Prestons' friends and said her goodbyes, surprised to feel such easy acceptance after a short amount of time at Quest Stables. The unquestioning welcome, the gracious attempts to make her feel at home, helped ease the transition from her friends and family back in L.A.

As she walked toward the foyer and the front door to leave for the night, she realized that if she wasn't so scared of the past following her, she would be throwing herself into her new life. She might even have explored the source of that steady regard in Robbie Preston's eyes every time she was around....

But that was foolish.

As her high heels clicked down the polished hardwood, she chided herself for thinking like that about a man who was not only a decade younger than her but also her employer's son. And besides that, since when did she think about the "regard" in any man's eyes? She'd barely looked at a carrier of the Y chromosome since—

"I tried to leave," Robbie announced, his long, lean frame unfolding from where he'd been sitting on a chair in the foyer. "But with the sun setting earlier and you being new in town, I couldn't let you navigate your way to your car on your own."

Shrugging, he offered her his arm and she stared at it for a moment, knowing this contact with him could be dangerous.

Then she gave herself a mental shake. Dangerous for *her* maybe. A gorgeous, wealthy male like Robbie Preston surely didn't feel the same pulse of awareness when they were together that she did. He probably had women falling all over themselves to give him a lot more than a little company for a stroll across the grass.

She was being silly.

Reaching out to him, she slipped her hand into the crook of his arm.

"Is this part of that legendary Southern hospitality I've heard so much about?" She kept her tone light, reminding herself that he probably viewed her as nothing more than a nice older woman. A mother. An employee.

He held the door for her and they stepped out onto the wide front porch. The stars were popping out as the cooler air greeted them. She pulled her shawl closer and warded off a sudden shiver.

"Actually, there are plenty of people who would argue that Kentucky isn't part of either the south or the north." He slowed his pace as she prepared to step down onto the front walk. "Southerners think this is the north and Northerners consider this the south, so we're in the unique position of not being claimed by either one."

Her heel hitched on a high spot as they stepped out onto the grass and she had no choice but to squeeze his arm to steady herself. Just for a moment.

Solid muscle lurked beneath his soft chambray work shirt. And yes, she only noticed that as a matter of curiosity. Robbie was a handsome man with a compelling presence and powerful physique—all things that any woman would notice, she hoped.

Then again, perhaps the cocktail she'd had with Jenna Preston's friends accounted for a hyper awareness that felt both embarrassing and uncomfortable.

"Well maybe it's not a north-south issue, but a Kentucky trait. I've been the recipient of amazing kindness since I moved here." She peered around the lawn looking for her car. There were many more people parked along either side of the driveway than when she'd first arrived.

"I'm glad to hear that." Robbie pointed out her compact car parked behind an exotic foreign number. "Is this you over here?"

"Is it that easy to pick out the hired help's cars?" She was definitely out of her element here. Although she'd been pleased enough with the outfit she'd pulled together from her closet tonight, she knew a converted bridesmaid's dress and a bargain warehouse lace shawl didn't give her the same style points as the women who moved in the racing world. At least she wore the same size she had in college and she favored classic pieces, so she had a few old dresses in her wardrobe.

The dresses she'd seen on guests tonight had been the kind women ordered off runways or—at the very least—snapped up in tony boutiques.

Robbie paused to peer down at her in the night now gone almost fully dark.

"I remembered seeing a car like this with California plates, so I figured it must belong to our only west-coast transplant." His forehead scrunched and she realized he was disappointed or perhaps upset that she had misinterpreted his words. "And I want you to know that an abundance of money has never been an indicator of anyone's character in my eyes."

His words soothed her even if she didn't want to admit she'd been a smidge intimidated tonight.

"Of course." She nodded quickly, all too aware of his presence beneath the rising luminescent moon. With the cool night air blowing around her skirt hem and brushing her shawl along her arms like a lover's fingers, she could almost get caught up in a moment she had no business being in. And sweet stars in heaven, what was the matter with her? "I couldn't help but notice every car but mine cost more than my last house. I hadn't counted on so much…*glamour* when I came to work at a Kentucky horse farm. It doesn't sound like such a sophisticated job on paper, but now that I'm here, I can't help but see a really different lifestyle than what I'd expected."

She released his arm, determined to extricate herself from whatever moonlight madness had taken hold of her tonight. Pulling the shawl tighter around her shoulders, she moved toward the car.

"Amanda?"

His voice halted her, the smoky warmth of it sliding down her spine and making her shiver.

If she didn't work for him—for his family—she would have damned the consequences of being rude and simply hurried away. She prayed the feelings he stirred up tonight were merely a weird by-product of all the changes in her life, the new faces and places, and being caught up in an evening where she was just a woman and not a mother. Her dress made her feel vulnerable, too aware of herself in a way that her chinos and polo shirts never did.

And what if this attraction was all one-sided? Maybe she imagined the response she felt in him. For all she knew, he could be silently laughing at her—or be totally shocked—because of their age difference.

Pausing, she dug for her keys in a tiny evening bag and waited for him to speak, her heels sinking into the soft bluegrass the longer she stood still. Would she sink into this place—this lifestyle—just as surely?

The Prestons' home glittered with lights as it sprawled across the lawn behind Robbie, and

Amanda suspected it would be all too easy to find new happiness here. If only she didn't have to worry about bringing trouble with her wherever she went.

"If you need any help settling in, I wish you'd give me a call." His dark-blue eyes held hers in the moon-light—and damn it, why did she have to remember his eyes were the exact shade of the Pacific right before a storm blew in?

Giving into a childish impulse, she squeezed her eyes tight for a moment to break the connection. Or maybe she needed to shut out the dark charm of this charismatic horse trainer who'd already won over her son.

Wrenching open her lids, she forced herself to smile. Nod. Tug her heels out of the earth so she could back up another step.

"Thank you, Robbie." His name felt too personal as she wrapped her lips around the word. "We're already feeling at home here, but I appreciate that."

Fumbling with her keys, she found the right one and inserted it into the lock.

"Thanks for letting me work with Kiefer on his riding. He's a great kid."

Amanda's maternal heart glowed with the small stroke of praise even as she hoped he wouldn't say more. It was bad enough she already felt an uneasy feminine response to this man. If he could appeal to the more fierce side of her—her motherly sensibilities—she'd be toast.

"It's me who should be grateful." One more nod. Smile. She sank into the driver's seat and lifted a cheery wave. "Goodnight, Robbie."

He probably returned the nicety, but Amanda lost herself in a whirlwind of activity inside the car. She shut the door, jangled her keys into place in the ignition and turned the engine over. She had mirrors to check and windows to look out—so long as all her focus was on backing up and not on backing away from Robbie Preston. Only when she was safely out on the driveway and ready to take off did she brave a quick glance at the man who had her wound so tight.

Sure enough his eyes were on her.

And just like that a jolt of pure, unadulterated feminine pleasure pulsed through her veins, making her feel more alive than she had in…a long time. Heaven help her.

Within the next second, she made the decision to stay as far away from Robbie Preston as possible.

Chapter Four

Amanda Emory should not have been on his mind.

Robbie waved to the exercise rider currently working with a claiming horse on the Polytrack outside the paddock. Nodding, the rider pressed the horse harder while Robbie forced himself to concentrate on his job. Normally, he prided himself on offering the lower-quality claiming horses and the allowance horses the same thorough attention he gave to the stakes horses that ran in the major races. But today, despite the strong workout from the focused filly, Robbie found himself remembering the worry in Amanda's eyes the week before when he'd walked her to her car. Tapping his pencil against his clipboard, he jotted some notes about the filly's increased weight and muscle definition. The new maturity really showed in her gait and confidence as she aced the breezing workout.

And why did Amanda seem more nervous than a yearling with a new trainer?

Jabbing his pencil back into the clip along the top of the board, he waved off the exercise rider and moved on to the next horse. A few fall leaves stirred around his feet despite the lingering warm weather. He'd been thinking about Amanda all week, unable to concentrate on his training programs with the same insight he normally brought to the exercise yard. A cranky owner had groused at him about something the day before—a confrontation that would have set him off at any other time, since this particular owner never put his horses' needs first—but Robbie had shrugged off the complaints easily since he'd been ruminating about why Amanda would be uncomfortable around him.

Because it couldn't be just about the attraction.

He knew she felt it the same way he knew she didn't want to feel it. He could read her body language the way he could read a temperamental filly's when she needed more exercise or a day of rest. That intuitiveness had created half the problems in his family relationships; he'd always been able to sense his father's disappointment in him even if Thomas didn't verbalize it, and that had made Robbie resentful from an early age.

So he didn't doubt that the awareness he felt was

fully reciprocated on her end. What he didn't under-stand was the source of her worry. He guessed the emotion ran deeper than any surface resistance to being attracted to him.

Amanda Emory was a woman of complex thoughts and feelings—the kind of woman he usually left well enough alone, since his life as the black-sheep Preston had been enough of a mess on its own. But like everything else about his connection to Amanda, that didn't make sense either.

"Are you losing your touch, boy?" a familiar voice called from behind him.

Robbie turned to see his grandfather ambling up the small rise toward the exercise yard, his worn jeans and long-sleeved plaid shirt never hinting at his multimillionaire status. Behind him, the spread of Quest Stables made a hell of a scene, the rolling hills and meadows in the distance, the bluegrass starting to dry out with autumn in the wind, the leaves starting to drop—a thousand acres of prime horse country.

At eighty-six years old, Hugh still liked to spend time around the stables—almost as much as he enjoyed checking out races around the globe with his horse-crazy cronies, guys who'd come up in the racing world along with him. But Hugh would have been as comfortable on a ranch out west as on a farm in Kentucky. As long as there were horses nearby, he was content.

Except for right now, it seemed.

"What's the matter, Granddad?" Robbie waved

to the colt's rider to initiate the workout while Hugh joined him at the rail.

"I saw you let that filly finish her workout without talking to the rider about how she felt from his point of view." Hugh raised a hand when Robbie started to protest. "I know you've got a schedule to keep, but that filly looked better than she has all summer."

Robbie staunched an inward sigh, respecting his grandfather's perspective. Besides, hadn't he been chastising himself for the same thing his granddad complained about?

"You're right." He nodded. Took his lumps like a man. At least Granddad said what was on his mind instead of letting problems fester beneath the skin.

Like his father.

"What?" Hugh frowned as he clapped Robbie on the shoulder. "No argument from the family rabble rouser? I thought you were always spoiling for a fight?"

Hugh's weathered face split into a grin and then the two men assumed the same position at the fence—one boot up on the bottom rail and arms folded along the top.

"How can I argue when you're right? I should have talked to the rider. But I did make a note to call the owner and let him know the filly is showing more promise. Her sire never brought much performance to the track, but this horse could be a whole different package."

The sun shone warm on his arms as Robbie tracked the colt now making the first easy laps of his workout. This was why he had got into training—the freedom to work outside and be his own boss. Except for the head trainer's occasional input, there was no one to tell Robbie how to do his job out here. Horses didn't argue. At least not in so many words.

"So, if you already know everything your old Pops came over here to say, care to explain why you're off your stride?" Hugh stole his clipboard to look over the notes Robbie had been making on the day's workouts.

Robbie never lied to this man. Nor did he hedge. It was a point of honor between the most outspoken men in the Preston clan that even when they were forced to control their tongues around other family members, they never bothered with such social caginess around each other.

Which left Robbie fairly tongue-tied at the moment.

"Ah!" Hugh's head popped up from the clipboard, his gray hair lifting in the breeze. "The eloquent sound of silence says it all."

Blue eyes twinkling, the older man gave a knowing grin.

"It's not what you think." Robbie didn't want to tread down this road today, not even with one of his favorite people.

"And what do I think? Give your grandfather some credit for having eyes, son. I didn't get as far as I did in this business reading horses without gaining a few skills in reading people, too. You've got the same talent as me, so you know what I say isn't just some trackside bettor blowing smoke." Hugh passed back the clipboard. "You should have told me you were having woman trouble and I would have understood exactly why you're off your game today."

Robbie jammed the training notes under his arm.

"I'm not having trouble with a woman." He had no business thinking about Amanda anyway. She just had a way of creeping into his thoughts when his mind was quiet.

And, if he was honest, even when it wasn't.

"Who is she? Some gal up in Twisted River you haven't bothered to bring around here?" Hugh pounded a fist on the fence post. "Damn it, boy, we don't know what's going on with you since you let your father chase you out of the house."

Here we go.

Robbie steeled himself for the battle.

"Granddad, you know we don't see eye-to-eye on this." He stared out at the training yard and caught sight of Melanie coming in on Leopold's Legacy.

Both men waved as she turned the horse in their direction.

"We *should* see eye-to-eye since I've been telling you not to let your father get under your skin since you were four years old." Hugh grumbled, groused and then put the subject away. "So help me, I want to meet this woman you've been thinking about. Do you hear?"

Robbie nodded absently because his grandfather would never let it go otherwise.

"How did he do today?" Robbie called out to his sister, envious of the way her duties as a jockey allowed her to ride far from the drama that always seemed to be circulating around the main house. His new set-up, residing in one of the staff cabins, might have removed him from the continual disagreements with his father and the rift between him and his brothers, but the arrangement brought new problems.

He had the distinct feeling it made the other staffers less at ease to have a Preston in their midst. There was a guardedness around the cabins now that had never been there when he used to pass by as a visitor.

"He ran like a champion." Melanie shook her head, her shoulders drooping. "He could be earning fat purses and the adoration of the whole racing community if it wasn't for this mystery about his sire."

A groom came over to take the reins from Melanie as she slid to the ground beside them.

"It's the damnedest thing I've heard of," Hugh declared, shaking his head over the issue that was never far from any Preston's mind these days. "I'll bet you any money it's some computer error. Back when we used to keep information in file drawers, people knew how to access it. Now that everything is done by computer, people don't know how to make their own damn breakfast without some bleeping machine telling them how to do it."

Robbie watched the groom walk away with Leopold's Legacy. Not so long ago, he and Melanie would have exchanged a wink over Granddad's tirade. But these days, they hoped he had a point and there was some computer error behind the discrepancy in Leopold's Legacy's blood work.

As Melanie launched into her ideas for clearing the horse to run in Dubai next month, Robbie's eyes snagged on a figure walking up a path from the stables toward the Quest offices.

A sweetly feminine figure he'd been seeing in his mind's eye all day.

"Would you excuse me?" He tossed out the question as a social nicety but didn't stick around for the answer. Plunking his training notes on a nearby bench, he stepped away from his sister and grandfather, his eyes glued to Amanda Emory and her tense body language.

With one elbow bent and her hand at her ear, she appeared to be on a cell phone. Her shoulders were rigid and her lips pulled into a taut line as she stalked past an urn of red flowers along the asphalt path that wound through much of the property.

As he neared her, she became aware of his presence and lowered her chin as if to keep her conversation private. He hadn't meant to intrude on a talk he had no business hearing.

Which made him wonder who she might be talking to. He'd never considered there might be someone else in her life. Someone she'd turned to after her husband's death…

And now he felt like a real jerk for barging into her personal life. He had backed up a step to leave when she pressed the off button on her phone and looked him in the eye.

"I'm sorry if I intruded—" he started.

Then he saw the expression on her face. The tense brow, the widened eyes, the skin paler than it should be.

"What is it?" He stepped closer now, automatically concerned by anything that would upset her. Their attraction aside, she seemed like a nice lady who'd been through too much.

He watched her tuck her phone into a pocket of her long skirt. She was back to work clothes today, a simple yellow blouse tucked into a red skirt with yellow tulips around the hem.

"It's nothing." She shook her head. Attempted a smile that wasn't one bit successful. "Some updates from my old neighborhood. I guess I was feeling a little homesick."

He gauged her tone and suspected there was some truth in the statement. He also suspected there was more to it that she wasn't telling him. Not that he had any right to know her personal business. He told himself to back off, even as he gestured toward the path ahead so that he could walk with her wherever she was headed.

"You're a long way from the west coast." He could almost feel his grandfather's eyes boring into his back as he headed away from the training yard.

No doubt Hugh Preston would assume Amanda had been the woman distracting Robbie today. And while that would be correct, Robbie hadn't made up his mind to do anything about it yet. And having his grandfather pushing them together or asking her pointed questions could make the work environment damned uncomfortable.

He had enough on his mind with his family's vote of no-confidence on the head trainer job. He didn't need to add complications to a personal life he'd done a poor job of managing.

"We lived north of L.A., but I was born and raised in Orange County. I was surfing by the time I was four." She seemed grateful for the change in topic and he was relieved to see the color return to her cheeks.

He had an image of her as a little girl, her dark hair sunkissed with highlights from long days in the sun.

"This must be a big change for you." He wondered if she minded being landlocked in America's heartland.

Her steps slowed as they neared the Quest offices.

"I really needed a major change." She tucked her hands in her skirt pockets. Right where she'd placed her phone. He wondered if she was thinking about that call again.

"Amanda—" He wasn't sure what to say. That he wanted to make sure she wasn't upset by that phone call? That he wondered if there was someone in her life? "Will you have dinner with me this weekend?"

The shell-shocked expression on her face told him she hadn't been expecting to hear that kind of invitation any more than he'd expected to issue it. He'd already told himself all the reasons it was best to leave her alone. Plus he'd seen her reservations about their attraction to each other.

Still, when someone monopolized a person's

thoughts the way Amanda had his the last few days, he couldn't imagine any way to deal with that besides spending more time with her.

"I don't think that would be a good idea." She turned to say hello to someone coming up the path— a woman who worked in the office.

He waited until she was out of earshot and then drew Amanda off to one side.

"Why?" He'd never been one to carefully weigh his words, and he couldn't start now. If Amanda felt pressured, he regretted that. But then again, he refused to let her ignore something that felt so incredibly obvious to him.

There was a spark between them. A connection that deserved to be explored.

"Why?" she echoed his question, but her tone suggested the answer was obvious. "For one thing, I work for your family. Don't you think that could be a little awkward when the day comes where you don't want to have dinner with me anymore?"

She fidgeted with a pleat down the front of her skirt.

"You work for my mother, not me." He knew his mother to be an objective and fair-minded employer. Actually, his father was too—when it came to anyone but his youngest son. "Are you seeing someone else?"

She blinked. Her hand stilled.

"I'm a widow." She spoke so softly that he knew he'd touched a nerve.

Ah, damn. He should have known that was part of

the reason for her reluctance to become involved. He'd have to tread more carefully.

"I'm sorry for your loss, Amanda." He reached for her hand and squeezed. "It's so unfair to you and your boys."

She nodded, as if accepting his comfort, but she slid her hand out of his.

"Thank you. It's been two years, but I haven't—that is, there isn't anyone else in my life." She tucked a windblown strand of her hair behind one ear, revealing side by side piercings filled with tiny gold hoops.

The revelation of that vulnerable part of her—the long expanse of her neck topped off with such a distinctly feminine decoration—made him want to reach out to her and protect her from life's hurts. Too bad right now it seemed like he was the one doing the hurting when he churned up the past.

"We could keep things—you know—low-key. No pressure." He just wanted to talk to her. Find out why she had needed a major change in her life. Discover her dreams for the future. Tell her all about the colt he saw so much promise in. Find out more about the woman who rode surfboards, something he wouldn't have expected from her given her reserved nature.

What other secrets might he discover about her?

"I can't." She stepped away from him, her dark hair sliding right back into place along her cheek. "Thank you for…seeing me as more than a mother or an administrator." She smiled. "It's been a long time since anyone has looked at me the way you do,

Robbie, and I'm flattered. But I can't offer you any more than friendship and a lot of gratitude for what you've done for Kiefer."

He had much more to say on the subject, but she brushed past him to return to the office building. Her job.

Damn it.

Melanie would say it was just his bruised ego that made him so upset about not convincing Amanda to see him. But there was more to it than that. As he watched her slender figure disappear into the building, Robbie recognized that she was lying to herself if she thought they could stay away from each other.

And he intended to help her admit the truth as soon as possible.

"Mom, Miss Heather said she'll take us on a tour around the parking lot to see all the painted faces. Can we go?" Kiefer stood at Amanda's elbow, his face desperate and expectant.

Max jumped up and down beside his brother, the younger boy's silent enthusiasm no less pressure for permission than Kiefer's pleading expression.

All around them, tailgating families and college kids swarmed the parking lot outside the University of Louisville's football stadium. It was a gorgeous fall afternoon, and music from car radios mingled with an impromptu jam session by a couple guitar players nearby. Kids ran pell-mell through the parked cars, carrying U of L pinwheels and Cardinals' foam footballs. The scent of barbecue sandwiches and hot dogs permeated the air.

Amanda had decided to attend the home game for the kids' sake, knowing she ought to show them the sights and help them fall in love with their new hometown after the trauma of uprooting and moving so far. Besides, the whole office shut down for the rare midweek game. Louisville was about forty minutes from the Quest facility, but a group of people from Amanda's office had been going, most of whom had kids. Heather was the daughter of one of the older women, a college student who was already loading up a couple of toddlers in a wagon for the trek around the parking lot.

"Can we, Mom?" Kiefer pleaded, casting a longing look around.

Amanda warred with herself for a minute longer, all the more protective of her boys since violence had intruded on her family. But the other women in the group were entrusting kids younger than hers to Heather, who was attending the university for a teaching degree.

"Okay." She hung on to Kiefer's arm for a second longer before he bolted. "But you help Miss Heather watch Max, okay?"

Heather drew the wagon closer. "I'll bet Max would like to ride in the wagon, wouldn't you, big guy?" She took the boy's sticky hand and led him to the red wagon decorated with the U of L fighting cardinal logo. "And Kiefer can walk with me."

Kiefer grinned up adoringly at Heather, whose sweet accent and mass of long dark curls made her a natural target for a young boy's affection.

Amanda watched the troop depart and helped herself to a soda from the cooler. Several of the women had brought lawn chairs and were seated around a small grill where they toasted marshmallows over the gas flame set on low. Amanda was weighing the idea of helping herself to a s'more when a familiar masculine voice spoke behind her.

"I'm not sure I could have dated a woman who was a Cardinals fan."

Amanda pivoted to see Robbie a few feet away. Dressed in a Quest Stables T-shirt, his muscles clearly delineated beneath the taut fabric and his face clean shaven, he provided too much temptation. His blue eyes glittered a warm invitation despite his words.

She'd barely managed to walk away from his dinner invitation. How would she withstand much more of his attention without running headlong into that brick wall of a chest? A woman would have to be blind not to be attracted to him. For that matter, her sense of smell would have to be defunct too, since just a hint of his aftershave kicked up her temperature lately.

"Is that right?" Amanda peered down at the red football jersey that one of her office mates had loaned her for the game. "Then I guess I saved you a lot of heartache by turning you down."

He sauntered closer, slowing to a stop as all her

coworkers turned as one toward them. From the knowing smiles scattered among them, Amanda could tell they all thought there was something romantic between Robbie and her.

Had he counted on that?

But by the way his grin turned sheepish, she didn't think that he'd banked on the curiosity. He said hello to the group and then took a few steps back, drawing her with him.

"Of course, I could overlook the U of L affiliation for football, as long as I can get you cheering for the University of Kentucky by basketball season." He looked so serious Amanda had to laugh.

"And do you get your way all the time, Robbie Preston?" She hadn't meant to flirt with him, although her words probably sounded that way.

"Not nearly as often as I'd like." He didn't crack a smile and the dark look in his blue eyes made the color rise in her cheeks.

Unsure what to say or how to break the spell he seemed to have her under, Amanda wondered if a woman could be hypnotized by the scent of after-shave and a man's compelling gaze.

"So what brings you to a Cardinals' game if you're not a fan?"

"I *do* like a good tailgate party." A wolfish grin spread over his face as he moved toward the bag of marshmallows and helped himself to one. "And I couldn't help but hear you would be attending. I thought I'd make sure you were shown the full range of the tailgating experience. It's sort of an art form around here."

He picked up a toasting stick and proceeded to give the marshmallow the rotisserie treatment.

Amanda turned back to look at the women she'd come with. They were standing in front of the lawn chairs now, and one woman seemed to be demonstrating a form of tackling, her stance wide, her elbows up.

"Well, I think we're only now getting around to discussing football. Mostly we've been grilling too much food, drinking some microbrews and discussing the betting pool at work."

Robbie nodded as he turned his marshmallow. "Impressive. Although you need a few more team flags on your car and some spray paint on the windows. And actually, I wouldn't mind seeing you in some red-and-white beads to match the jersey. Possibly sunglasses with a logo painted on. When I talk you into that UK hoop game with me, I'll make sure we do it up right."

Amanda laughed. "Anyone ever tell you that you're incorrigible?"

"Never with that particular adjective, but I believe I've heard the same general verdict, yes."

A football flew between them and bounced against an SUV. Amanda scooped it up and tossed it back to a pair of apologetic teenage girls.

"But it doesn't bother you if you occasionally come across as...oh, say...pushy?"

"Life is too short not to go for what you want. If

I get shot down, I'm okay with that. But at least I don't have to live with a case of the 'what ifs.' " Carefully balancing his marshmallow stick with one hand, Robbie reached into the back pocket of his jeans with the other and flashed a handful of tickets at her. "I've got some fifty-yard line seats for you and the boys. I'm willing to root for the Cardinals for the day if you'll share the afternoon with me."

Amanda's mind was still processing the bit about life being too short.

He couldn't have swayed her more effectively. She'd raged at the heavens over the unfairness of that very thing in the months after her husband died. She'd been working hard to keep the boys' life on an even keel, trying to hold all the pieces together for their sake.

But what about stealing some fun for herself?

"Did you already buy tickets?" he prodded as Heather and the boys came into view and caught sight of Robbie. He didn't even notice, too busy assessing the golden color of his marshmallow.

Kiefer would be beside himself to hang out at the football game with his new horse-trainer hero. Her son was already putting his shoes in motion.

"We didn't buy tickets since we were going to get the cheap seats at game time." She looked back at Robbie and hoped she was making a good decision. "Maybe we could watch the game with you if we can keep things—you know—just friendly?"

She hated to sound scared of him—of what spending

the day with a man might mean—but she couldn't deny being nervous. If she hadn't already said yes, she would have changed her mind five times already.

Grinning, Robbie leaned down to give Kiefer a high five while Heather pulled the wagon a few yards behind. Robbie removed his marshmallow from the stick with practiced care.

"In spite of what you may have heard about me, Amanda, I promise I can be plenty friendly." He handed Kiefer a ticket and then leaned closer to Amanda to pop the toasted marshmallow in her mouth.

The warm sweetness of the treat melted over her tongue as her resolve died away.

He didn't wait for an answer. Then again, with her mouth full of marshmallow, what could she say?

He grinned. "I won't disappoint you."

The timbre of his voice—"for her ears alone"—produced an immediate fluttering inside her chest.

And heaven help her, she felt certain he wouldn't.

Chapter Five

*J*ust *friends.*

Robbie waited for Marcus to show for a morning meeting, remembering Amanda's dictate at the football game. He didn't need to review his training notes for the meeting since his main news for Marcus was that he wanted to step up training for Something to Talk About—news that wouldn't be well received. So, as Robbie lingered over the coffeepot in the staff room behind the stables, he thought about how hard he'd worked to play by Amanda's rules. Even later that night when he'd taken her home, he'd been nothing but a gentleman at her front door. Of course, he'd needed to be a gentleman in front of her kids. Would he have been so committed to holding back if he'd been alone with Amanda? He honestly didn't know.

Pouring a cup of some gourmet-smelling fancy brew his sister must have made, Robbie couldn't help but wonder what would happen if he got Amanda alone. And yeah, he wanted to. He sipped the coffee to shake off the chill of the fall morning. Before the U of L game, he'd figured that if he spent more time with her, maybe he'd quit thinking about her all the time. But if anything, the opposite was true.

He only wanted to know more about her. The woman fascinated him for a hundred reasons. She'd shunned college to backpack around India and she'd rebelled against her family, who'd rigidly controlled her life until she was eighteen. She'd moved into a communal house near the beach with six other kids to surf and figure out what she wanted in life and met her late husband when he had busted a roommate for drug possession.

Robbie hadn't learned much else about the guy, but he had discovered Amanda was a diehard Dodgers fan and remembered the smallest details about some of the biggest plays the team had made in the last two decades. Her recounting of injured Kirk Gibson's home run during game one of the '88 World Series had amazed him. Even though he wasn't big into baseball, the sports fan in him recognized her love of the game and admired it.

Admired her.

Hell, he was in deep.

"Robbie." Marcus entered the room from the door connecting the staff areas to the stables. He didn't bother with a greeting other than a brief nod as he helped himself to a cup near the coffeepot.

"Marcus." Robbie shoved aside thoughts of Amanda as best as he could, already knowing he wasn't going to honor the "just friends" dictate now that their impromptu date was over.

"I got your workout notes from last week." Marcus sniffed the coffee as he poured himself a cup. "What the hell kind of brew is this?"

Robbie shrugged. "It's Melanie's stuff. I think she switches to some pumpkin-spice thing once she decides it's autumn."

Marcus took a swig, his face screwed up like a kid trying brussel sprouts for the first time. He swallowed, shrugged. Drank a bigger swig.

"So, do you care to explain why you want to rush the training for Something to Talk About?" Marcus tossed a pile of papers on the table, sending empty packets of sweetener flying.

Robbie recognized the memo he'd written about bumping up the workouts for the colt.

"I'm not rushing him."

"He's undersized. You know it can be risky to push a horse who hasn't matured and filled out." Marcus sent him a hard look as he tossed the empty coffee cup into a recycling bin.

"And you know that determining a horse's readiness to race doesn't rely solely on quantifiable data."

Robbie sensed the horse's determination. Recognized the animal's hunger to compete. "I know the colt is ready for more. If we wait, we risk missing his peak racing window."

"How can you tell?"

"Sixth sense. Damn it, Marcus, you know I can't define it in so many words. There's a twitchiness in him, a restless energy. I think he's ready to prove himself."

Marcus frowned, clearly not appreciating the absence of hard facts.

"I'm sure you know it's my head that will roll if we spend time and money on a horse that isn't ready." Marcus eyed him shrewdly, no doubt wondering if Robbie was trying to sabotage his career.

"Believe me, I would like nothing better than to be able to put my own head on the block for this and every other decision about the training programs at Quest. It's no secret I wanted your job. But I can't tailor my training recommendations to be more conservative now. I'm telling you what I recommend and you can take it or leave it. But bottom line, that horse needs to step up his workouts now."

Melanie walked into the room just then, her riding gloves in hand. She was sweaty and a little dirt-streaked. No doubt she'd come in from a hard ride.

"I can come back—" she started.

"No." Marcus cut her off. "We're finished." He scooped up his notes and turned to Robbie. "I'll schedule in the extra time for the colt, but if he doesn't begin to show some serious—quantifiable—

progress within two weeks, we need to taper off until he's filled out."

Stalking out the door that led outside, Marcus left them alone. Melanie broke the silence with a soft curse.

"That felt tense." She approached the coffeepot and put her gloves on the table before pouring herself a cup in the ceramic mug she stored in an overhead cabinet. "So who are you training harder?"

"Something to Talk About." He didn't feel like defending his decision to his sister any more than he'd wanted to defend it to the new head trainer.

"Ah." She nodded as she sipped her coffee, her eyes momentarily closing in appreciation. "And speaking of something to talk about, I've got a doozie."

"Is that right?"

"Is it true you introduced mom's new office manager to Cardinals' football?" She smiled over her coffee cup as she let the steam drift off the brew to swirl around her face.

Robbie tensed. Not because he cared if Melanie knew about the date that wasn't a date, but he wondered if the fact that gossip spread fast around the stables would discourage Amanda from seeing him again.

"What does it matter if I did?" He'd never minded people talking about him. Most of his choices in life had generated discussion inside the family and out. But he hated the idea of making Amanda a topic of water-cooler conversation.

"It's unusual for you to date anyone involved with Quest." She eyed him in that knowing way women had when they questioned men about other women, and it made him uneasy.

"It's unusual for me to date anyone involved in aerodynamics too, but that doesn't mean I'd discount a woman who's involved in the field."

Melanie plunked down into a wooden rocking chair near the table. She began a slow, methodical rock, the chair squeaking rhythmically.

"Okay. But it's also unusual for you to date a widow. With two children. Who also happens to be— what? A decade older than you?"

Robbie crushed his coffee cup in his fist and pitched it into the bin like a fastball.

"What the hell difference does it make if she's a widow or has kids or—any of that? Do you have a point here, sis, or are you trying to tick me off by focusing on a bunch of superficial stuff?"

She lowered her coffee and whistled between her teeth.

"Point taken. I'm sorry if that came across as being superficial and it's not my business. I just hope you know that a woman who mom thinks has been through a lot—a woman with two kids to think about—is bound to look at dating a lot differently than you."

Robbie swallowed a curse and wondered if his day with Amanda was now up for family discussion, but he was too disgusted to ask if the topic had come up over dinner the previous night.

How did his family get the idea that he would be so immature about relationships? At least now he knew he had to be on guard if anyone asked him about Amanda.

"I'm well aware of that, Mel." Robbie couldn't wait to get out of the staff room and start his work.

He'd had all the second guessing he could stand for one day—from his sister *and* Marcus.

"She seems great though, Rob." Melanie called after him as he made his way to the door. "Even if she does root for the Cardinals."

He cracked a smile as he stepped out into the yard, knowing his sister had only meant well. She'd been trying to give him a heads-up on what the family would have to say about Amanda and he appreciated that.

Especially because he'd never been one to think about the consequences of his actions before. But maybe, if he could anticipate some of Amanda's concerns before she tossed them back in his face, he'd be one step closer to making her say yes to his next proposition.

Because "just friends" wasn't going to cut it in his book.

Amanda stayed late on Friday night to work on the file reorganization, knowing she was avoiding going home as much as she was sorting out Quest's information systems. It would be different if the boys were around, but they'd begged to attend "fun night" at the after-care program, and since Amanda had been rooting for them to really feel at home in Kentucky, she hadn't had the heart to ask them to stay and keep her company.

Lately, sitting around her house in the evenings after the boys went to sleep, she felt like a fifteen-year-old waiting for her first boyfriend to call. Which, of course, was beyond screwed-up since she'd made it very clear to Robbie she didn't want that kind of relationship with him anyway. But something had happened when she'd spent the day with him last week. She blamed it on sitting next to him for hours on end, being on the receiving end of accidental brushes of his hand or the occasional rub of his shoulder against hers when he leaned down to hear something she said.

Apparently some component of her body chemistry had shifted into overdrive ever since the mass exposure to Robbie Preston's appeal. She had become exquisitely responsive to even the mention of the man's name in the days that followed. She found herself daydreaming about what it would be like to touch him—taste him—in the middle of the afternoon while she was at work. When one of the other women in the office had dissected a date she'd had over lunch the day before, Amanda found herself thinking about what might have happened if she'd allowed Robbie to direct the course of their day together instead of holding back so firmly.

As it was, the night after the football game, Amanda had spent the hours before dawn lying on top of her sheets since even the slide of high-thread-count cotton had irritated her flaming skin. Her dreams had been wildly inappropriate and had made her blush all day long.

Tilting back in her office chair, she allowed herself a glimpse around her cubicle. A large and spacious affair that was as private as any office save Jenna's, the space had been decked out with racing memorabilia before she arrived. Commemorative plaques hung on the taupe walls, recognitions of Quest's charitable works and corporate sponsorships. But Amanda's favorite part of the office decor was the old-fashioned use of horseshoes hanging over every doorway.

Forcing her attention back to her computer, she stared at the file for Leopold's Legacy. It would be a mammoth undertaking to organize, and since she liked to work in alphabetical order, she really needed to tackle the controversial Thoroughbred's documents next. She checked her watch, knowing the kids' fun night at the after-care program would only last another half an hour. She didn't have time to start on the file tonight.

Shutting down the computer with more than a little regret, she made plans to ask Jenna for wider work access through her home computer since she could have worked well into the night on the project. And who knows? Maybe she'd find something helpful in the horse's records that could clear up the mystery surrounding his sire.

Gathering her purse and tossing a can from an empty diet drink in the recycling bin, Amanda shut lights off behind her as she moved through the office building. Jenna was working late on something so Amanda waved as she went by her office.

She had barely left the building when she ran into Robbie.

Figuratively speaking, of course. She stopped like a treasure hunter with a beeping metal detector well in advance of seeing him, her whole body now sensitive to his presence. When he emerged from the shadow of a few trees near the darkened path, she still gasped with soft surprise at the powerful pull she felt.

That chemistry should have grown weaker with time apart, not stronger.

"Hi." She straightened the strap of her purse to cover her confusion and hoped the dark hid any hint of flushed cheeks.

Yup. She'd so regressed to a fifteen-year-old where he was concerned. She'd have to go to a hypnotist or something to eradicate such juvenile behavior from her repertoire. Except then she'd have to actually describe her embarrassing behavior to another human being and that—

"Amanda." The way he said her name made it sound like the answer to an important question.

Or was she indulging her inner dork with thoughts like that? God, she'd sucked at dating the first time around until her husband simply strode into her life and clarified everything for her, making marriage seem like the most obvious answer in the world. Maybe without Dan to help her she'd suck all over again.

Oddly, her late husband's brief appearance in her thoughts didn't distract her from her heated skin or the fluttering of her heart in her chest.

She and Robbie stood in silence for a long moment that should have felt awkward, but didn't. Amanda could have stared up at him for hours if it wouldn't have interfered with picking up her boys.

"Come with me." He broke the silence, sliding an arm around her waist just long enough to set her in motion beside him.

His touch disappeared a second later, making her wonder if her overactive imagination had dreamed it.

"I have to get the boys—"

Robbie checked his watch. "Claudia has the kids out on a hayride with Fred through the old pasture. If you try and grab them now, I guarantee your oldest will argue you out of it anyway."

His understanding of Kiefer surprised her into a laugh as her steps shadowed Robbie's down the asphalt path that wound around most of Quest's outlying buildings. She could smell a bonfire on the breeze, the scent of burning leaves sweet and acrid at the same time.

"Do you think I'm too indulgent?" She dared any man—even one who appealed to her as much as Robbie—to critique her parenting. She was proud of her sons and thought she did a damn good job with them for the most part.

"I don't think you're too indulgent by half." He grinned, his teeth a flash of white in the dark as they walked away from the office toward the staff cabins where Claudia lived. "But I've seen Kiefer in action and he definitely hones his reasoning skills on you.

I think you could get him to leave with you, but you'd be exhausted by the effort."

Amanda considered the comment and decided she couldn't be terribly offended since he was quite accurate about her son.

"So where are we going if it's too early to pick up the boys?" She checked her watch too, but without an illuminated dial she couldn't see what time it was since the trees blocked the moon.

He turned to her, a movement of rippling muscles she felt more than saw.

"We're going to my place."

Chapter Six

"Isn't that a little presumptuous?"

Amanda's defensive instincts leaped to the fore even as a shiver of awareness ran over her skin. She wouldn't simply fall in line with this man's plans for seduction, even if—

"We won't go inside," he promised, his hand making a brief appearance on her back to steer her forward. "My cabin is right near the path where Fred will take the kids on the hayride. You'll have a front-row seat to wave at them as they go by."

"Oh." How perfectly reasonable. Thoughtful, even.

She ought to be relieved Robbie was a gentleman who didn't force this issue of dating with her.

So damn it, why did she experience a sudden twinge of let-down?

"There's a patio heater and a couple of chairs outside." He pointed down the path to the left as they came to a fork in the walkway. "We can watch the stars until the wagon goes by."

"That sounds nice." She really needed to dust off her manners around him and stop being so defensive. "Thank you."

They walked along in companionable silence for a little longer, passing a half dozen small buildings painted white like most of Quest's outbuildings. Amanda loved how sharp the whole property looked. The fresh coats of paint must be updated every year to maintain their crisp brightness. When they reached a small cabin with a porch light burning, Robbie slowed his step.

"This is my place. The patio is around back, but if you don't want to get your shoes wet, we should walk through the house to get out there."

She nodded, knowing she couldn't afford to ruin her shoes when the relocation to Kentucky had dug deep into her savings. The move would be worth every cent and more if it kept her and the boys safe, but Kevin, her husband's former partner, had called during the week to give her an update on the movements of Benny Orway, who'd been released from jail.

While Amanda appreciated the officer's vigilance on her behalf, every call he made only reminded her that she might never be able to stop looking over her shoulder.

When Dan had shot one of the gang's members, it was like taking a shot at the whole gang. Even though Dan was killed too, his enemies were apparently numerous and not even his kids were exempt from the gang's hatred and vows of revenge.

"Are you cold?" Robbie asked her as he opened his front door and gestured for her to go inside.

Only then did she realize she was shivering.

"Maybe a little," she acknowledged, grateful for the excuse of the weather. The days remained warm in mid September but temperatures were starting to cool off when the sun went down.

"I'll get that heater cranking outside." He led the way through the small cabin which looked as if it might have two bedrooms off the main living area. The walls were left unfinished, the warm, knotty pine coated with something to give them a high gloss even under the dim overhead light he'd switched on. The furnishings were simple and definitely not the kind she would have associated with someone from a family as wealthy as the Prestons. The light fixtures were wrought iron and the sofa was made of a durable canvas that looked comfortable and inviting. Bright rag rugs were carefully rolled up to one side of the floor.

"Have you been vacuuming?" she couldn't resist asking, curious about his lifestyle. Most men with so much wealth and privilege wouldn't feel the need to live in a residence intended for workers.

He scooped a blanket off the back of a barrel chair near a sliding-glass door and then flipped on an exterior light.

"No." He grinned as he held the door for her and escorted her over to an Adirondack-style chair on a cobblestone patio. "I keep the floors clear so I can dribble the basketball through the house. Keep my game up."

She laughed. "All you need now is a rim over the fireplace."

He laid the blanket across her lap and then moved toward the tall, stainless-steel patio heater. Flipping it on, he made the lights glow warm before he wheeled it closer to her chair.

"Great idea. Just think what an indoor rim could do for my hook shot." He hesitated near the other Adirondack chair. "Can I get you anything to drink?"

She shook her head even as she realized how easy it would be to get comfortable here. With him.

A pleasant shiver replaced the clammy fear she'd experienced earlier.

"No, thank you." She spread the blanket out on her lap, touched by this symbol of his thoughtfulness as she breathed in the scent of a nearby bonfire.

He drew another chair close to hers, the arms inches apart, and took a seat. She could see him more clearly now under the porch lights, his khakis and polo shirt a change from the stable T-shirts and jeans he wore when training horses.

He looked very, very good.

"I'm surprised you don't live in the main house." She flipped the tassle of the blanket he'd given her, stroking over the navy-blue wool.

She'd heard he was a hothead and that he didn't get along with his father, but she didn't place any stock in hearsay. Especially not after all the problems she'd had pleasing her own family. No doubt her father's friends would have categorized her as a wild child and possibly, by association with the friend who was arrested, a druggie.

She'd never touched a non-prescription pharmaceutical in her life, but since when had the truth ever squelched a good rumor?

"I did up until a couple of weeks ago." He tipped his head back against the wide slatted boards of the weathered gray chair, his hand drooping off the wide arm of the seat. "But some bad vibes have escalated with my family ever since I got passed over for the head trainer job."

She stretched her limbs out along the arms of her chair too, watching the way their bodies aligned in such close proximity. If she extended her hand toward him just a fraction of an inch, they'd be touching.

"You should have asked Kiefer for a reference." She glanced over at his profile in the moonlight and her breath caught in her throat at the sight of him. She couldn't deny her attraction. "He thinks you walk on water when it comes to horses."

Robbie grinned. "That's because he's only just

meeting me now. My father has the benefit of remembering when I wasn't so disciplined with the training. I once took his fastest Thoroughbred out for a midnight ride to work off some restlessness and brought him back with a cut on his flank from a branch I didn't see. Plus, the unscheduled exercise mucked up his training schedule and—well, mostly I could have really hurt the horse by riding at night and not on the track."

"How old were you?" Her hand brushed his.

An accident? Before she could pull back, he gripped her fingers.

"Fifteen." He squeezed her hand lightly and didn't let go. "But I only proceeded to make more dumb mistakes for the next three years. I had a case of teenage brain-freeze or something."

Warmth traveled up her arm and seemed to suffuse her whole body. She thought she should probably disengage her hand from his long, strong fingers, but she didn't move an inch.

"You speak as if that's a rare disease." She couldn't count all the stupid things she'd done between sixteen and twenty.

She'd had a lot of fun though. And she didn't regret any of it.

"It is in the Preston house." His thumb stroked the back of her hand. "My brothers were born brilliant, athletic and wise enough to think before they opened their mouths. Andrew and Brent were a tough act to follow as business manager and breeder and—quite frankly—I didn't have any interest in being a carbon copy of either of them."

Amanda bit her lip at the heat firing up inside her at the slow slide of his thumb over her skin. She lifted her gaze to the moon to distract herself from the warm intimacy of talking to Robbie in the dark.

"So what other crazy things did you do in your youth? I'll bet you didn't surf in unknown waters or dance in public fountains with your friends, did you?"

His head whipped around to face her.

"Not you."

She grinned. "I was a southern California girl living the dream."

He shook his head. "I still bet I've got you beat."

"Try me."

"I got kicked off my school hockey team when another player hit me and I went ballistic. I made the school debating team but then embarrassed my whole family by going off on a politically sensitive rant that I won't bore you with now. My debate was so radical, it was published in the local paper in full, unexpurgated detail."

"A source of pride for you and further resentment for your father, right?" She stroked his hand lightly.

"Bingo. But then I turned down a scholarship opportunity to law school to go into horse training, which my father was convinced I'd never succeed at. I worked two jobs off campus to pay for the classes for the first two years until my mother made him agree to kick in a portion. But I guess that wasn't bad behavior. It was sort of smart since I really didn't want to be a lawyer."

"Come on, Robbie. Dig for the juicy stuff. You hurt an expensive horse and got in a hockey brawl. I still say I've got you beat. I moved out before I was eighteen and it took you until you were how old?"

"Twenty-eight."

"My point exactly."

"I gave away a potential racehorse to my first girlfriend."

Amanda laughed. "I think that's wildly romantic. But hardly the act of a brash hothead. I'm wondering where you get your reputation from, Robbie Preston?" She turned to look at him again and he leaned forward in his seat, propping his elbows on his knees as he seemed to search the darkened horizon for answers.

His hand was still wrapped around hers.

"I think it comes from my arguments with my dad. We've never seen eye to eye. It's like I was born with all the wrong instincts—or at least instincts that run contrary to every last one of his."

The troubled expression on his face called her to move forward in her seat too.

"It's strange how you never fully get out from under those relationships that are so pivotal. I talk to my mother and my sisters all the time, but things will always be strained between my dad and me. He wanted his last child to be a boy and he got me. He's been disappointed since that very first day, but there isn't a damn thing I can do about it."

Robbie's gaze connected with hers, hot and focused. He tightened his grip on her hand with a gentle squeeze before he released her.

"I'm really glad you weren't a son." His fingers lifted to touch her cheek, stroking lightly over the cheekbone and the hollow underneath.

Amanda's breath grew heavy in her chest and she felt as though her lungs expanded forever, the moment as drawn out as that breath.

She opened her mouth to speak, unsure what she was going to say. She never had a chance, however, because Robbie's mouth inched closer to hers. He moved so deliberately that she had plenty of chance to say no. To stop. To run away.

But not for the world did she want to interrupt the steady progress of his smooth, sculpted lips toward hers. The moon and the man had her hypnotized.

Robbie watched Amanda through half-lowered lids.

He wouldn't push this. Wouldn't push her. But damn, hadn't he given her every chance to wave the "just friends" flag?

Curving his hand around the back of her neck, he guided her closer and brushed his lips over hers. Gently. His whole neurological system lit up like a switchboard on overload. He drew his fingers across the silky nape of her neck, unleashing the clean scent of her shampoo. Her lips molded to his like ice cream on a hot afternoon, pliable and sweet. He could have tasted her all day.

All night.

He'd spent so long thinking about her, imagining what it might be like to kiss her. Now that he had her here, her kisses throwing fuel on a fire that had been lit long ago, he wanted to drag her into his lap and hold her whole body in his arms.

He wouldn't. Couldn't. But by the saints, he wanted to know what she'd feel like cradled against him. He breathed in her scent, her vanilla fragrance mingling with the shampoo, and he wanted to nudge aside the collar of her blouse to taste the base of her neck. Inhale her there.

His fingers combed through her dark hair while he reached to touch her with his other hand. Those fingers landed on her collarbone, right where he wanted to kiss her next.

"Robbie." She spoke softly against his mouth, the vibration of the words against his lips a seductive tingle that made him crave harder pressure.

"Mmm?" He released her mouth but descended to her jaw line, tattooing her skin with kisses the whole way down. If she had any plans to stop him, he would at least milk every last taste of her he could manage until she expressed as much.

"You shouldn't want me."

That wasn't "no" in his book.

Licking a path down the column of her neck, he reached her collar and inhaled. More vanilla. The scent was stronger here. Sweeter. And drove him wild.

He wouldn't even be able to stand after this kiss, his body was so rock-solid for her.

"Wanting you isn't up for debate. It just is." He could prove to her exactly how much he wanted her, but he was moving slowly, damn it.

Gently.

He forced himself to ease back a little, to take a moment and breathe in the scent of her where he'd kissed her. To trail a finger down her throat and savor the rapid beat of her pulse beneath his touch.

She surprised him by cupping his face in her hands and turning his mouth back to hers. The kiss she laid on him was anything but slow, and not exactly gentle.

He loved it.

She grazed her tongue along his teeth and pressed closer to him, despite the awkwardness of the chair's wooden arms. A thready sigh hummed up her throat and her fingers speared into his hair. His thoughts fried and his focus narrowed to getting her inside, in his arms, possibly underneath him. The need for her roared in his ears after being suppressed for weeks, the sound growing louder. Stronger. Impossible to ignore.

Amanda pulled back, as if she heard it too.

What the hell?

"It's the wagon," she whispered, her eyes filled with panic as she drew away. "The kids."

She recovered faster than he did, scrambling away from him just as the hayride party came into view. A camp lantern swung on one of the slats of the high wagon, the light swinging back and forth with the easy clip-clop of an old field nag that Fred used for this job year in and year out. The ranch hand was good with kids and volunteered for the riding club and any youth activities around the stables.

Robbie liked him well enough, but he wasn't exactly thrilled to see him now.

The group was singing "My Old Kentucky Home," one of Claudia's favorites. She'd been running the after-school-care on the premises for as long as Fred had been driving the hay wagon, and the song was a standard for this event. The kids who weren't singing were laughing and squealing, their hands stuffed with candied apples Claudia had given out for a snack.

Robbie didn't bother standing up to wave, convinced he might be lightheaded enough from that kiss to fall over. Amanda was on her feet and blowing kisses to Kiefer and Max, however, her maternal smile so beautiful that he wished he'd been the guy responsible for giving her the kids that made her so happy.

And *whoa*. Where in the good green earth had that thought come from?

He blinked his way through the fog of thwarted lovemaking—well, at least that's what it had been at his end. Maybe for Amanda it had been no more than a thwarted kiss. But at least he'd gotten his chance to prove to her that there was undeniable chemistry between them.

Chapter Seven

"You must like him a *little*," Kiefer insisted in the car on the ride home that night. "You went to his house. Remember? I saw you there."

Amanda remembered all right. Her skin still tingled with the warm memory of Robbie's touch, her mouth pleasantly swollen from his kisses. Sweet stars above, she had never expected to feel that way again.

Now, after picking the kids up at Claudia's, Amanda drove back to her condo in Twisted River, the dark country roads deserted in this part of Woodford County. She kept her eye out for deer that were on the move at this time of year—or so she'd been told. Mostly, she just kept her eye on the yellow line since there were no lights to illuminate the roads here.

She'd had an abrupt parting with Robbie after the hay wagon passed by. Abrupt. Ha! She'd practically sprinted out of there in her hurry to put aside all the feelings he stirred in her, feelings she feared were even more powerful than those she'd had for Dan.

And that scared her. It also felt downright disloyal.

She didn't have the slightest idea how to proceed next since none of the problems she had where Robbie was concerned had gone away. He was still younger, still her employer's son. Still a single man who'd never had children while she—she came with a lot of history and two great kids whose happiness she wouldn't risk on feelings that made her uneasy.

"Yes, baby, I know. Mr. Preston was nice enough to offer me a spot to watch the hay wagon so I could wave to you and Max." Her gaze went up to the rearview mirror to see her youngest slumped in his booster seat, his eyes closed and mouth open in sleep.

The sight made her heart constrict. She wanted to keep her boys safe, the responsibility for them double now that she was a single parent.

"So why don't you like him enough to be his girl-friend?" Kiefer cocked his head sideways to meet her gaze in the mirror for a split second before her eyes were on the road again.

"Kiefer, it's not that simple." She lowered her voice to make sure she didn't wake up Max since the last thing she needed was a second matchmaker involved in this conversation. Her scalp itched with protest at the topic. "And while I love you to pieces,

I would rather not talk about my possible boyfriends with you, okay?"

"But Robbie *could* be a boyfriend, right? You said it's possible?"

Dear, sweet, merciful heaven. It was as if her mother and sisters had brainwashed her son into this role before they'd left California. He sounded *exactly* like them whenever they'd harangued her about her dating status over the last year. Kiefer simply wouldn't let up.

"Kief, I'm the adult and I'm in charge of the boyfriends." She risked a glance in the rearview mirror to give him the low-level maternal warning glare. "But I promise if I decide that's what I want, you'll be the first to know right after me."

"What about Max?" Kiefer turned to look at his brother, tilting his head low in front of Max as if to check if he was really sleeping.

More maternal heart twists. She was still so sad for Dan that he didn't get to share these moments of watching his sons grow.

"I don't know. Do you think Max cares about my boyfriends?"

"Nah." Kiefer grinned at her in the mirror. "He's still just a kid."

Amanda smiled as they drove out of the darkness and back into the relative civilization of Twisted River, a community of about twenty thousand people. Lights dotted the road again, guiding them until they reached the turn-off for the small, gated community that provided as much security as Amanda could afford right now.

Even as she greeted the night guard and used her pass key for entry, she thought about what Kiefer had said, his teasing implication that he wasn't a kid even if Max still was.

There was some truth in that, and it hurt her to think that Dan's death and her struggle to cope with single-parenting had forced Kiefer to grow up faster. But she wouldn't compound that problem by putting him through the pain and disappointment of her failed relationships. She wouldn't risk having Kiefer get too attached to Robbie only to have his idol sail out of their lives when he realized all that he'd be sacrificing in a relationship with an older woman who had two kids.

That was a kind of growing up she could spare Kiefer.

Of course, it meant ignoring the most intense physical attraction of her whole life. Avoiding Robbie Preston and the feelings he'd stirred inside her wouldn't be easy, but it would be better than the alternative of picking up the pieces for her—and Kiefer—after he left.

"Robbie Preston, I'd like to speak with you right this minute."

Robbie turned from his workout with Something to Talk About to stare down at his mother.

She stood in the middle of the corral yard, her feet

in leather boots instead of her office shoes since it was the weekend. A week had passed since his kiss with Amanda and it felt as if she'd gone into hiding. She hadn't returned his phone calls and she was nowhere to be found around Quest. Of course, she had to be at work every day, but Robbie wouldn't invade the sanctity of her workplace—yet. He'd thought she would have made an appearance by now, even if it was just to say she realized the other night had been a mistake.

"I'll be done with the workout in ten minutes." He had been making good progress with the colt but Marcus hadn't given him much time to show a marked improvement, so every workout counted. "I can come find you as soon as I'm finished."

His mother folded her arms, her slight frame taking on a more formidable posture. A cool breeze blew her auburn hair around her face, the autumn chill creeping into the air when the wind kicked up. The horses loved the cooler weather and Something to Talk About was no exception.

"Oh, you'll come find me? I'd rather go back up to the main house but since you refuse to set foot in it, I guess I'll just wait here until you finish."

O-kay. Robbie knew better than to rile his mother when she was in a very rare mood like this one. She was known all around Quest for her sunny disposition and hospitable ways, but Robbie had a special knack for needling the nerves of even the most patient of souls.

"No need, Mom. I'll get someone to take over." He whistled to one of the exercisers coming in on another horse and passed Something to Talk About over to her along with a few quick instructions.

By the time he turned to his mother again, she had unfolded her arms and some of the sternness had left her face.

"Sorry for the interruption, Robbie." She walked with him to the far side of the corral, away from the handful of staff in the yard. "I've been wanting to talk to you all week, but you never come around anymore and by this morning I'd gotten myself worked up over it."

Robbie could sense the tension in her and was sorry he'd been the cause. He put an arm around her and bent down to kiss the top of her auburn waves. His mother had a soft heart and she'd run interference for him with his father often enough when he was a kid. But bottom line, she sided with his dad when push came to shove, and it wasn't entirely unwillingly. She didn't agree with Robbie's choices and he'd never been enough of a persuasive type to make her see his side.

"I'm sorry, Mom." He steered her toward a wrought-iron bench with a carved figure of a horse's head in the middle of the back. "I'm doing my best dealing with being passed over for head trainer, but I think it's easier if Dad and I don't have to play out our frustrations every night at the dinner table."

The arguments weren't usually about training, but

the fact that he and his father never saw eye-to-eye on anything under the sun made it tough to have a meal in peace. Robbie had moved back into the main house after college in the hope he could mend fences with his family while working at Quest, but he didn't have that assurance anymore. He'd buy his own place before he went back.

"Robbie, even aside from all the issues between you and your father, you have to admit that you are young for that kind of position. Not just at Quest, but any operation of this size."

"Marcus is only four years older than me. Daniel was only four years older than me. Is that such a substantial gap? And I did train Leopold's Legacy. That should count for something." Robbie shook his head, unable to hold back just one more comment from his perspective. "You know I have a considerable advantage with knowing every horse in residence on a personal basis. It'll take Marcus years to even come close to the kind of—"

He cut himself off before he got too wound up.

"You know what? I don't want to argue with you, Mom. Is there anything I can do to make you happier about this situation? How about you come over for dinner one night and I'll show you the new place. I do a mean steak on the grill."

She pulled her sweater tighter around her, her hands rubbing warmth into her arms. "I can't go to your house for dinner without your father. Can't you at least come up for cocktails one night a week?"

The ground in front of them rumbled with the thunderous hooves of one of the bigger, older Thoroughbreds out for exercise. Bit O' Barley was a descendant of Old Barley, Hugh Preston's first champion racehorse. The original Barley had been the financial foundation for Quest Stables, even though the operation was named for Clara's Quest, the very first horse Hugh had claimed and won at Aqueduct Racetrack in 1941.

"Cocktail hour is when ninety percent of the strained conversations that turn into arguments occur." Damn it, he wasn't getting roped into that.

"What if you come with Amanda?" His mother waved at the exercise rider on Bit O' Barley as the former champion made another lap.

"Mom." He could imagine there'd been talk about them after so many of Amanda's coworkers had seen them together at the U of L game. He hoped that hadn't made trouble for Amanda.

"What?" She turned back to look at him, a warm sparkle in her eyes as she smiled. "I really like Amanda and so does your father. She seemed to enjoy cocktails with us, in fact."

Frustration simmered inside him. Not at his mother, but at the whole damned situation. He shouldn't have made his interest in Amanda so well-known around Quest.

"Amanda is great, and I'm sure she enjoyed hanging out with you and dad. But she's made it clear to me that we're going to be just friends."

Her disappearing act this week reiterated her

position more clearly than words could have. She must regret kissing him. Touching him. Giving free rein to that spark between them, if only for a short time.

"Maybe she's just unsure of herself, Robbie." His mother reached for his hand, as she had when his first real girlfriend in eleventh grade had broken up with him. "I'm sure it's awkward for her to start a relationship with a member of the family who employs her, and she's got kids to think about, so she has to be all the more cautious."

He gave his mom's hand a quick squeeze and then released it, unwilling to discuss Amanda.

"I'm sure she has plenty of reasons not to get involved with someone like me, so rest assured there won't be any cocktail hours with Amanda on my arm."

Damn it.

But before his mother could try to fix that problem too, he stood.

"That invitation for dinner is always open though. And I never said Dad wasn't invited. If you can drag him out of his kingdom for a night to mingle with the working class, you know where to find me."

"Robbie." His mother called him back before he'd taken two steps.

He turned.

"We can't afford more divisiveness around here when the questions surrounding Leopold's Legacy's sire are already threatening to shake the very foundations of Quest." Jenna stood, striding closer, meeting his gaze head-on.

"You think I should offer an olive branch just because times are hard for the family?" The Prestons would survive the crisis no matter what became of Leopold's Legacy.

Robbie knew everyone at Quest was afraid of the consequences. The revelations that Leopold's Legacy was not sired by Apollo's Ice, the horse on record, called into question the integrity of the stables. Breeders wouldn't buy Quest's horses and owners wouldn't want their horses boarded here. Already some owners had pulled out. The ramifications could be huge.

"I'm suggesting that your father is a hard man who doesn't understand you, whereas you're a hard man who understands people very well. I would never ask you to compromise your professional goals for the sake of this family, Robbie, but I would ask you to consider bending your personal boundaries for the sake of a little harmony."

He didn't know how to answer that one. In fact, he wasn't fully sure what his mother meant him to do. Did she expect Robbie simply to excuse his father's cutting comments and dismissiveness where he was concerned?

"Good luck with the colt, Robbie. Melanie says Something to Talk About is really coming along well." His mother stretched up on her toes and kissed his cheek before she walked away.

Robbie stood beside the corral for long moments after she left, thinking about what she'd said. There'd been a time when he would have argued the point about caving to his father's needs, but in the weeks since he'd met Amanda he found himself weighing his words. Or, at least, giving himself time to consider his actions before he said what came to mind.

It had started off as a reaction to being continually distracted by thoughts of Amanda. But today, he found himself actively holding back with his mother because he didn't want to drive a wedge deeper between himself and his family. And not for his sake. No, he'd been thinking about Amanda and how his mother had said they liked her.

Silly, really, since he probably wouldn't ever have a chance to bring Amanda around for the cocktail hour that was a Preston tradition. Still, he understood that a woman like Amanda was committed to family. What would she think of him if he wasn't even on speaking terms with his own father?

Robbie glanced back at the big house and his mother walking in the distance. He breathed in the scent of dried leaves and the hint of fall on the breeze, then laughed out loud at himself.

Amanda didn't know it, but she made him a better man. Too bad she didn't want any part of him.

Should he leave her alone and give her time to realize what they were missing out on? He had the feeling that a woman's willpower was a force to be reckoned with. And why make it easy on her? He'd head over to her place today and plant himself in her path.

As it happened, Kiefer had been begging him to

intercede with Amanda about a horseback riding camp on the ranch anyway. Robbie had a made-to-order excuse to see the woman who'd invaded all his dreams.

Chapter Eight

Thank God for weekends.

Amanda had sent up the prayer of praise more than a few times since she'd driven off Preston property at quitting time on Friday. Now, as Saturday morning crept into Saturday afternoon, she remained grateful for the time with her boys—time away from the powerful presence of Robbie.

"Mom, we're going to shoot baskets at Nathan's house, okay?" Kiefer shouted through the front door.

He and Max had been playing with their neighbor at the condo all morning and Nathan's mom had promised to take the afternoon shift so Amanda could get a little work done. Jenna had sent a CIS technician to Amanda's place earlier in the week to set her up with a work account on her home computer so she could continue her file reorganization from the comfort of her house. Jenna had offered incentive pay for the extra project and Amanda was more than happy to sneak in some work around the boys' schedules.

"Okay, hon. Make sure you say thank you to Mrs. Braden." She padded around the condo in her pjs, her favorite apparel on the days she didn't have to work. They were sufficiently decent loungewear—blue cotton pants and a T-shirt with a pattern of duck-lings—that she wasn't embarrassed if the kids' friends came through the house.

Something about wearing pjs all day made her feel leisurely. And given the things she had to worry about lately—Benny Orway's release from prison, the safety of the boys now that they were chomping at the bit for a little more independence, the slow, subtle pressure from Robbie to take their relationship into hotter terrain…

Yes, she needed to relax.

Stepping over a pile of pick-up sticks and a Lego fort full of plastic dinosaurs, she plunked down on the red leather couch that dated from her very first apartment and cracked open her laptop.

She'd finished Leopold's Legacy's file last week but failed to find any clues about what had gone wrong with his siring. Now she was up to the *S* files and closing in on the *T*s. It wasn't rocket science, but the neatly compacted folders on her screen gave her satisfaction. If only life fell into such orderly compartments.

She hadn't finished college but returned to night school to get the computer certification she needed to put herself on the job market quickly after Dan died. She'd planned to finish her college degree through distance learning programs while the boys were in grade school, perhaps studying accounting or something business-related. But Dan's death had altered those plans and her dreams of staying home with the boys for as long as possible. She'd given surfing lessons to help supplement Dan's income, and those days out on the waves had been just enough to appease her need to get out of the house for short stretches....

God, she couldn't afford to live in the past anymore.

Anger at herself bubbled up out of nowhere. Forcing her focus back on the laptop, she knew Robbie's presence in her life was the reason for this sudden habit of revisiting the past.

Was she hiding in it? Or was she going through all her old memories as a way of putting the past to bed? That option scared her even more since it meant she'd have no choice but to face the future head-on.

A knock sounded on the door and she wondered if Kiefer had locked himself out. Come to think of it, she should always keep the door locked, even if the boys weren't in the house with her.

"Who is it?" she called, suddenly worried that it wasn't Kiefer. That Benny Oray hadn't shown up for his meeting with his probation officer and he'd come for her.

"Robbie."

The sound of his voice made her legs weak. With relief it wasn't Benny? Or with a purely feminine response to a man who undid her with no more than a glance?

Her hand paused on the door knob.

"Do you think this is wise?" she asked softly, her forehead tipping against the wood panel.

"I thought you'd rather talk here than at Quest." His voice sounded low and close to the door, and she wondered, if the barrier wasn't there, how many inches would be between their faces right now?

But he had a point about it being better to talk here. She knew her relationship with Robbie had already been cause for office gossip. She opened the door while taking a quick inventory of the house. The dinosaurs' fort and the half-folded basket of laundry. The television she'd forgotten to shut off in her haste to get to work after the boys left. Max's half-eaten toast on the counter. Perhaps this scene of single-parenthood chaos would send Robbie running for good.

He stood on her doorstep dressed in a gray suit with the jacket unbuttoned. He wore a crisp white shirt and a cerulean silk tie that brought out the blue in his eyes. He looked different than she'd ever seen him, a far cry from the horse trainer in jeans and T-shirts who kept to the stables instead of the offices or the main house.

Now, with his hair sleek from his shower and his face freshly shaven, he appeared every inch a Preston—wealthy and powerful.

She backed up a step to search for the remote and kill the inane chatter of the television, feeling more than a little self-conscious in her duckling pajamas.

"Sorry about the mess," she offered, shoving the plate with the half-eaten toast into the sink.

"I'm the guy who plays hoops indoors, remember?" He grinned and leaned into the doorframe. "So do you mind if I come in?"

"Please do." She hurried over to the sofa to clear a place for him to sit before she retreated to the safety of a chair on the opposite side of the room. Gesturing to the couch, she tucked her legs up under her. "You look nice."

Not that she planned to throw herself at him. But a man who took time to wear cufflinks around town deserved the praise. Despite the slightly juvenile nature of her weekend attire, Amanda loved sophisticated clothes. The Prestons' cocktail party had been a fun chance to play dress up.

"I had a meeting with a local breeder about some joint business down the road." He ignored her offer to take a seat and stooped to look at the Lego fort. "Where are the boys?"

"They're at a neighbor's for the afternoon." It was just as well Kiefer didn't see Robbie here, walking around their home as if he belonged there. In their lives.

Still, Amanda could have used the natural buffer of children with this man around. She felt vulnerable wearing her nightclothes in the empty house.

"The dino crew has an amazing pad here. I especially like all the choices of doors and windows they can go in and out."

He checked the hinges on a couple of the windows.

"They need all the shelter they can get when Max and Kiefer decide to play T-Rex and stomp anything in their path." The boys had earned more stubbed toes and scratched feet that way, but the accumulated battle scars didn't seem to deter them from a favorite game.

"Cool." He rose but still didn't move toward the couch, his blue eyes roving around her messy living area.

She'd covered the white walls with the boys' artwork, so construction-paper masterpieces were the main decorating theme. Robbie's eye went right to one of Kiefer's drawings, a picture of a horse with a short writing assignment beneath it.

"'Robbie Preston knows everything in the universe about horses,'" he read aloud, then went silent as he finished the last few lines detailing Kiefer's hero's amazing ability to understand all kind of horses and to train them to be their best.

"I told you he could have written you a reference." Amanda straightened a pillow in the chair beside her and her cheeks went warm as Robbie was confronted with the role he already played in Kiefer's life. "He thinks the world of you and I really don't want to give him false hope that there is anything going on between us. He got the wrong impression the other night at the hayride when—"

Robbie crossed the floor in a split second, his long strides easily covering the length of the room.

"He didn't get the wrong impression." Robbie dragged over an ottoman and lowered himself in front of her chair so they were at eye level. "He sees the same thing everyone else does when they look at us together, Amanda. There's a connection."

Her heart picked up its rhythm at his nearness, a testament to the truth of his words even if they were damned inconvenient. The attraction between them only made things complicated.

"I have to think about the kids, Robbie. I won't drag them through a relationship where they're bound to get attached to you."

"Why is that a bad thing?" He leaned closer as if he could press the idea home. "Kids form attachments to teachers and babysitters, neighbors and horseback-riding instructors all the time. Why not me?"

"They've already lost their father." Her eyes burned even as her arms ached to wrap around Robbie's broad shoulders. "I can't allow them to go through the pain of losing a father figure, too. And I don't care how careful we are, that's what will happen if we spend any more time together. Kiefer is already asking why we aren't dating."

"Damn it, Amanda. You haven't even given us a chance and you already have us broken up and the kids hurt."

Robbie tried not to be angry at the way she'd tossed aside any chance that he might stick around.

He'd come here to ask her for more, but she'd made up her mind that she wanted less.

"The boys have been through too much for me to take that risk now." She sounded so damn sure of herself, but her eyes widened if he got close to her, and she licked her lips if his gaze strayed toward her mouth.

He'd bet his inheritance that she didn't know she did it. But those small gestures, those sweet indications that she wanted him too were driving him crazy. And not just because he wanted her badly. Those small habits meant she was denying herself what she wanted for the sake of problems that hadn't happened yet.

"You're borrowing trouble." He hadn't touched her up until now, but sitting here, this close to her, he couldn't resist any longer. He laid a hand on her knee, the cotton fabric soft against his palm as he absorbed the heat of her. "And what if I can be a good friend to your kids now and in the future, no matter what that future might hold?"

Had she bought into the idea of him being a hothead after all?

"I don't know."

"Will you think about that as a possibility?" He stroked his hand lightly along her leg, a persuasive caress.

"Why?" She tilted her chin at him, her question a challenge.

"What do you mean *why?*"

"Why me?" She sat straighter in her chair, although she didn't protest his hand on her knee. Her dark eyes flashed with an inner fire. "You could have your pick of women all over Woodford County. For that matter, you've traveled all over the country for horse races. I'm sure you've met some of the most beautiful and elegant women in the world. So my question to you is, why is it so important that a forty-year-old widow with two children goes out with you? Haven't you turned enough heads already?"

The words shot out so fast and furious he was almost surprised by the silence that hung in the air following her question. Since when did he let incendiary remarks go unanswered? He was feeling pretty damn fired up himself.

"You think I care about how freaking beautiful and elegant the women in my life are?"

Her eyes widened as he realized how that sounded. Damn it, he needed to think before he spoke.

"That didn't come out the way I intended. You're a beautiful woman, Amanda, but that's not why I'm interested in you." He was incensed that she questioned his attraction to her, miffed that she'd blown him off all week and downright offended that she had him pegged for the kind of guy who would run roughshod over her kids' hearts after some kind of down-and-dirty fling.

"No, I think you got it right the first time because I'm not in the same category as the kind of people I met at your mother's cocktail party. Look at you, for example." She waved vaguely at his suit. "The whole world you inhabit is something straight off the set of *The Bold and the Beautiful*."

"I spend most of my time checking out horse's haunches. Does that sound elegant to you?" He looked down at his hand on her knee, his fingers digging into the fabric, gripping *her*. "And to answer your question, I wanted you at first because of pure, undiluted hot chemistry, and I felt that from the very first moment I laid eyes on you."

He could feel the mood shift in the room—hers as much as his. Her lips parted.

"But the more I'm with you, the more I realize I want you because you're smart and hardworking. You're a great mom and you have a really easy way about you that makes it nice to be around you. You have an encyclopedic knowledge of the Dodgers that I find impressive, and you're a sharp dresser with the kind of clothes I find myself fantasizing about removing."

Her tongue moistened her lower lip.

"The pajamas aren't my best effort," she admitted, although her eyes said something a hell of a lot more interesting.

She stared at him like a woman who wanted more than a kiss.

He reached for her the same moment she reached for him. There was a sudden tangle of arms and elbows, a clash of limbs and hunger. When it settled out, she was on his lap and in his arms, her lips pressed to his.

He held her there, one hand stroking up her back and the other gripping her hip to keep her balanced on his thighs. She was an armful of soft woman and sweet promise. Robbie's fingers couldn't be still on the thin cotton of her pajamas, his hands wanting to soak in the feel of her curves and warmth.

She sighed into him—not with a sound but with her action. He didn't know what she'd done with all that steely resistance of hers but it was gone for right now and he planned to make the most of every second that she remained willing and eager against him.

Mouths fused, he tightened his grip on her and pulled her hip deeper into his lap, her breasts flat to his chest. She made a little hum of pleasure in the back of her throat, her fingers shoving his suit jacket off his shoulders.

Sensation rocked him, blasting his body with heat. He skimmed his hand beneath her pajama top to find creamy soft skin at her waist and her belly. His fingers rose higher and her breath snagged in her throat, her nipples beading into tight points he could feel right through his shirt.

He cupped the weight of her breast in his hand, teasing the taut crest with his thumb. She arched her back, breaking their kiss as a slow sigh hissed between her teeth.

Tugging off her shirt, he lowered his mouth to one tight pink nipple, drawing on her. She gripped his shoulders, holding on to him and steering him at the same time. He let himself be guided, taking one breast and then the other into his mouth, flicking his tongue over the tips.

She worked his tie off, sliding the silk from under

his collar before she unfastened one button after another on a steady path down the front of his shirt.

His skin flamed as he held back the urge to lie her down somewhere, anywhere. He wanted to stretch out over her and peel the rest of her clothes away, but he wouldn't rush her. Couldn't push her any more than he already had.

"Robbie." She cupped his chin to encourage his glance, her lips damp and swollen from his kisses. "I can't stop myself, but we should slow down."

Her fingers fanned out on his abdomen, her touch so damn close to where he needed it most. He felt too light-headed to think. But his body had a hell of a better plan than his head right now anyway.

"You're asking *me* for restraint?" He shook his head at the irony of it, but some emotion sneaked through the passion-fog long enough to appreciate her faith in him.

Amanda might be the first person he'd ever met to assume he could demonstrate patience.

"I'm having a hard time holding back where you're concerned and I have—" She broke off, shaking her head as she managed to insert a small amount of space between them. "I have to."

He heard the words but couldn't act on them yet. The best he had to offer her was to hold still, because disentangling himself from her…every cell in his body protested the thought.

Her phone rang. A peal of insistent tones that sounded like a bell signaling the end of this round.

He'd be lucky if he could take another go in the ring like that, his body so keyed up he couldn't wrap his brain around trying to walk out of here.

"Excuse me." She scooped up her pajama top and held it to her chest before she slid off his lap. "I should check just to make sure it's not the boys."

As she headed toward a phone in the kitchen, Amanda's hips swayed, her pants riding low enough to give him a glimpse of the pink lace panties she wore beneath. Her bare back set his mind off on all the ways he could tantalize her from behind if she would stand still long enough to let him…

Ah, damn.

He could stand under his showerhead set to Numb for the rest of the day and he still wouldn't be able to shake this fire in his blood for her.

"Hello?"

He could hear her pick up the phone and turned to watch her where she stood near the refrigerator, its door covered with more art projects held on by a bunch of Dodgers magnets.

"Hello?" Her voice sounded tense.

Angry?

He hit his feet and crossed the floor, his instincts humming a warning.

Amanda moved the phone away from her ear to stare at it, her face pale as she looked down at the display for the caller ID number.

"Is everything okay?" He stepped onto the cool

tile floor beside her, his arm going around her automatically.

He could see the screen flash *Unknown Caller.*

"I paid to have the kind of service that blocks calls from unknown numbers." She thumbed the off button with extra force and he could have sworn her fingers shook.

"Are you getting obscene calls or something?" He'd like to set up camp right in front of the microwave to answer the damn phone a few times and put an end to that.

"No." She shook her head and replaced the handset in its cradle. "Just a few hang-ups."

Her voice sounded more steady, but her skin remained pale.

"Are you sure it's not telemarketers?" He slid his hand along her spine, worry for her holding his desire in check more than anything else could have.

"Maybe." Turning out of his touch, she held the shirt to her more tightly. Her eyes had gone cool again, although he couldn't tell if she'd simply remembered her reservations about their relationship or if she was worried about something that he didn't fully understand.

"Amanda—"

"I'm sorry." She brushed past him into the living room, pulling her shirt over her head as she walked. "I'm just at a point in my life where I need some more time before I can jump into things."

He thought about the weeks that had gone by

since they'd met. This was the longest he'd waited for any woman.

"You think we're jumping into things?" Perhaps she'd heard the frustration in his tone because she glanced his way, her brow furrowed.

"I should get dressed before the kids come home."

In other words, she wanted him to leave. Robbie pulled his shirt off a chair and slid into it.

"I'll go." He couldn't get a handle on the vibe in the room, but he knew something was off. Part of it was her own hesitation about starting something with him, but she had to see they'd not only started something—they were up to their eyeballs in it.

But now he wondered if there was more to it. An old boyfriend who called her? Some piece of her past she was hiding? He didn't know, but he resented the hell out of whatever it was that drove her away from him.

He buttoned his shirt and slung the tie around his neck, knowing there was a drink in this town with his name on it.

Possibly three.

"You know the stables are sponsoring an overnight horseback-riding trip next week?" He had to at least follow through on his promise to Kiefer to ask Amanda about it.

"Kiefer has mentioned it a few dozen times, yes."

"If there's anything I can do to help assure you that he'll be safe with Fred—"

"Kiefer has to miss this one. Maybe next time." She didn't sound like a woman who would change her mind any time soon, but Robbie sure as hell couldn't figure out why.

But then, he hadn't been able to put together many of the puzzle pieces where Amanda Emory was concerned.

As Amanda held her section of chilly ground on one side of the living room, he opened the door to leave. Tossing his jacket over his shoulder, he had the feeling he wouldn't ever be back.

Chapter Nine

"You need to report it to the local police."

The advice from Dan's former partner confirmed Amanda's instincts later that day as she spoke on the phone in her condo. She hadn't been sure if running to the cops over a couple of hang-up calls seemed paranoid or smart, and she was grateful for another point of view. Because even though she received updates from the L.A. probation department about Benny Orway's whereabouts and she knew he had to stay in California, she wouldn't leave anything to chance where he was concerned.

She wouldn't be able to straighten things out with Robbie until she felt completely secure in her new life with the kids. Not until the last two years had she realized what a blessing it was to feel totally safe. She'd never take that feeling for granted again.

"Do you think they'll do anything to find out who's making the phone calls, or will they just make a note of my complaint so there's a record of it?" She couldn't deny a small measure of angst over the idea of talking to the local police. As much as she admired the men and women who were called to serve and protect, she knew there would be plenty of memories associated with walking into a precinct full of blue uniforms.

"They should do both. With any luck, they can alert the local phone company so you can have a way to contact them quickly after a hang-up. Once they have the system in place it's easy to trace a call." Kevin had been patient with her fears, never failing to take her seriously.

"But as far as you know, Orway is still in California and meeting with his probation officer regularly, right?" She knew Kevin would contact her immediately if he thought otherwise, but after another hang-up call, Amanda craved whatever reassurance Dan's former partner had to offer.

"He's been checking in every week, just like he should. And I've got everybody on the force keeping their ears open for any news from Orway's gang about his movements or for rumors of any sort of revenge plot."

Amanda wandered into the hallway outside the boys' room and plunked down on the floor so she could be nearer to them as they slept. Hearing about gang plots and vengeance wasn't making her feel better.

"Thank you." She squeezed her eyes shut for a long moment, willing a note of strength into her voice. "I'll call the police in the morning and file a formal report. I appreciate everything you've done for us."

"Dan would have done the same for Katie and my kids." He paused and she could hear some kind of shouts in the background—a new arrest coming through the doors maybe. "Are you settling in okay out there, Amanda?"

She knew Kevin wasn't exactly a talkative guy so she understood he was making an effort to be nice. To stay connected despite the two thousand miles separating them now.

"Everyone has been really nice." Amanda recalled Robbie's eyes right before he had kissed her, and her belly did a back flip. She'd *definitely* been welcomed here. "If only I didn't have Orway to worry about, I think I could be happy here."

"We'll keep any eye on him." After a few more pleasantries, Kevin was off the phone and back to his own life, leaving Amanda to wonder how she could sleep at night knowing that bastard Orway might have already found her here.

Upset with herself for not setting up some kind of line-tapping system with the phone company before now, she slipped into the boys' room to make sure the windows were locked. They slept on the second floor, their windows facing the street, which would make it more difficult for anyone to get to them here. They probably faced greater risks at school or at after-care.

Still, Amanda went into her room to retrieve her blanket and a pillow so she could sleep in their room until she could alert the police tomorrow. She would buy extra locks for the windows and doors. Having been married to a cop for fourteen years, she knew just the kind to purchase.

Tucking herself into the blanket she'd brought, she kept the phone close by as her eyes adjusted to the dark. She took comfort in the measured breathing of her sleeping sons. Although, truth be told, she might have taken more comfort from Robbie's presence in her condo tonight. Stretched out beside her...

She needed to stop thinking about him and focus on what was most important in her life right now. She'd never resented Dan's job when he was alive, and even after his death she'd found some peace by reminding herself that he'd always said he wouldn't want to be anything but a cop. His skill as an investigator and his selfless need to protect others had made him an ideal police officer and he'd understood the risks.

But not until right now had she fully appreciated those dangers. Because even though she'd come to terms with Dan trading his life to take down a dangerous drug dealer, she hadn't understood that terrible price wouldn't be the ultimate sacrifice. Dan would be furious to know his family might still be at risk when he wasn't around to protect them.

The dangers of his job had chased him beyond the grave. No matter how much she craved the romance and companionship Robbie Preston offered, Amanda couldn't relax into her new life here until she was certain her children wouldn't suffer because she'd let her guard down.

"I think what we need is some fun and frivolity around here," Jenna Preston announced during an office meeting the following Monday morning. "So I hope you're all planning to attend the fall stable party and harvest gala on Saturday."

A little hum of approval went through the assembled group and Amanda put down her pen to listen. She'd been so focused on her own agenda for the meeting, she hadn't been paying full attention to the rest of the proceedings.

Of course, ever since she'd visited the local police station she'd been more distracted in general. The Twisted River police had been great, coming out to her condo to do a walk-through and suggest security measures she could take, plus they'd contacted the principal at the boys' school and Claudia at the aftercare program to put them on alert. The boys now had safe words in place and Amanda had a system for reporting her hang-up phone calls.

But still, she felt restless. Uneasy. Lonely for a certain blue-eyed man who didn't understand why she needed to back off. She owed him better than that, but she'd been rattled after the phone call

Saturday and she hadn't wanted to delve into her private fears. She'd simply wanted to get her boys back under her roof and put in a call to Kevin to make sure Orway was still two thousand miles away where he belonged.

That didn't make it right to shut Robbie out.

And really, she needed to let more people at Quest know about the potential threat Orway posed. She'd thought moving across the country would protect her from the ex-convict, but since the hang-up calls were continuing even here, she saw no choice but to make everyone aware of the potential dangers. She'd draft a memo with Orway's mug shot to circulate to the office staff so others could be on the lookout.

"For those of you who are new to the Quest family this year—" Jenna's gaze paused on Amanda "—we encourage everyone to attend the party in the afternoon with your family. There's apple-bobbing and pumpkin-carving for the kids, along with face-painting and pony rides. There's a hay maze and a bonfire for the adults, plus we have square-dancing lessons in one barn and a regular dance floor with a band in another."

One of the women leaned over to Amanda and laid a hand on her arm.

"It's so much fun. Your boys will love it."

Amanda nodded, but she was distracted by a sudden vision outside the office window—Robbie and Marcus were in deep discussion by the corral. Trainers and stable staff didn't attend weekly office meetings, so Amanda had known Robbie wouldn't be in the conference room today. Seeing him now, even if it was a hundred yards away, made her pulse flutter.

God, she wanted to run out and see him. Throw her arms around him. Tell him she was sorry for ending their time together so abruptly over the weekend. But she had a presentation to give today and a meeting she should be paying more attention to….

She could see she'd need to attend the fall stable party even though she was trying to keep a lower profile at Quest—both to help her stay strong where Robbie was concerned and to make sure the boys were with her as much as possible. But she couldn't live in fear, either. She would bring Kiefer and Max to the party.

Would Robbie attend the gala even though his parents were hosting the event? Her eyes traveled to the window again, her gaze roaming over his long legs and broad chest. He'd have to mend fences with his family at some point given his position at Quest. Then again, maybe he wouldn't. The man had such strong ideas about his horses and their training that maybe he would simply walk away from the family empire to start his own training program.

Not that that was any of her business, she reminded herself. She'd given up the chance to have an opinion on the subject when she'd drawn her boundaries so damn tight they didn't include him.

A fact she already regretted, even if she didn't know how to handle the situation any other way.

"Ladies and gentlemen, I'm counting on you." Jenna glanced at each individual at the oversized conference table. "Quest has suffered financially since we lost the ability to compete in the big national races and I've noticed we've all been a little tense around here lately. So I'm hoping we can shake off our worries this weekend and have a great time because we *will* find a way to come back, stronger and better than ever, from this mix-up with Leopold's Legacy."

Spontaneous applause broke out around the table and Amanda joined in, her hopes for the Preston family going deeper than a mere display of support for her employer. She genuinely liked the people at Quest and she owed Jenna Preston the world for taking a chance on her when Amanda had no experience and so little to recommend her for this job. As much as Amanda might worry about her safety and that of the boys while they lived here, she couldn't imagine what a nervous wreck she would be if they were still in California.

Amanda would gladly do whatever she could to help Quest thrive, even if that meant socializing with a man she was nervous about seeing. A man she wanted to see so desperately she hurt.

The meeting broke up a few minutes later and Amanda gathered her things. Her presentation on the new computer filing system had been postponed until after lunch, so she had a couple of hours to work on other projects until then. She thought about going out to look for Robbie, but he'd already disappeared from the corral.

"Amanda." Jenna signaled her to stay in the meeting room as everyone else filed out.

Assuming Jenna wished to discuss her upcoming presentation, Amanda joined her at the head of the table.

Jenna tucked one folder into another as she scooped up her papers, her wedding rings winking under the fluorescent lights as she moved.

"I hope you don't think this is presumptuous of me," Jenna began, sliding her folders into a leather portfolio. "But I've had a hard time catching up with Robbie lately and I wondered if he's attending the gala. Do you happen to know if he'll be there?"

Jenna looked weary. Or worried, perhaps. Amanda wondered if she was suffering more from the strain of the Leopold's Legacy scandal or from the rift between Robbie and his father.

"I haven't spoken to him about it." She wasn't sure what else to say since she didn't know if she would see him before the stable party either. She was meeting with the condo manager about installing extra security today, and the rest of the week was full with the school open house and an appointment with a contractor to upgrade the locks.

Jenna nodded. "I'm sure I'll catch up with him soon. I'd just heard that the two of you were seeing each other and thought maybe—"

"We aren't." Amanda wanted to squash the rumors with Robbie's mother even though she hadn't bothered trying to shut down the rumor mill in the rest of the office. "Seeing each other, I mean. He was kind enough to get some great tickets for a U of L game a couple of weeks ago, but—we're at such different points in our lives."

She knew that didn't exactly explain where things stood between her and Robbie, but she felt certain Jenna wouldn't want to hear all the details, either. Plus she didn't want to upset the boss. Just because Robbie didn't mind the possibility of dating a forty-year-old woman didn't mean his family would approve. What would Jenna think of her if she started seeing Robbie?

Jenna adjusted a colorful mother's ring that she wore on her right hand.

"I'm sure that wouldn't bother my son." She gave Amanda's arm a quick squeeze. "Not that it's any of my business, Amanda, but I hope you don't think for a moment that Robbie would care that you have kids or that you've been married or anything like that."

Amanda shook her head, feeling awkward. But Jenna charged ahead.

"My son has encountered most of the problems in his life because he says exactly what's on his mind and acts according to his own wishes. That quality can be an awkward one in business and even in personal relationships, but the up side to his personality is that you always know where you stand with him. Believe me, if he'd had any reservations about a relationship, he would have told you exactly what they were."

Amanda stared into the other woman's eyes, surprised to be having such a frank conversation. Perhaps Robbie hadn't pulled his habit of speaking his mind out of thin air.

"It's not Robbie's fault—"

"That's okay, dear." Jenna moved toward the door, shaking her head. "You don't owe me the slightest explanation, I just thought I'd check with you about the gala. And as a mother, I couldn't resist throwing in my two cents about my son. It's an old habit I should definitely break."

With a wave, she was gone.

Amanda sank into the nearest chair. She wasn't just hurting herself by keeping away from Robbie. She was hurting him, too. He'd admitted he was attracted to her at first because of chemistry, but then he'd gone on to list all the other ways he was drawn to her.

His words had turned her inside out as much as— more than—his kisses. And if Jenna was right, Robbie had meant every last word of that declaration.

Her heart ached with want and she knew she had to find a way to apologize for the abrupt way things had ended over the weekend. She might not be able to dive into a real relationship with him, but she could offer him a dose of honesty too. He deserved more from her than half truths and avoidance.

"Have you seen Amanda?"

Robbie had fielded the question way too many times for a man who hadn't even shared a real date with the woman. He'd seen her from a distance at the festival earlier that afternoon with the boys, but he'd been pressed into service giving pony rides and hadn't been able to speak to her before she disappeared.

Now, ten minutes after his arrival at the fall gala—his first entrance into his parents' home since the night he'd sought Amanda's permission to teach Kiefer to ride—Robbie turned to face the latest in a long line of people who'd expected to see Amanda on his arm tonight.

His sister wore a floor-length purple gown, her fair hair held back from her face with an amethyst clip in the shape of a horseshoe. Her perfume smelled clean and sweet, but Robbie had been hoping for a whiff of vanilla and a glimpse of the woman everyone around Quest expected him to be with tonight.

"I haven't seen her." He snagged a glass of champagne from a passing waiter's tray and took a swig.

It wasn't the same as smooth Kentucky bourbon, but it would tide him over until he made his way to the bar.

"So what do you think of the gala?" Melanie looked around the room, a vast parlor connected to a living area that had been cleared for the event. The wall was a set of giant pocket doors that could be slid back for large events, something Quest hosted often when times were good.

And while times were far from good now, Robbie's mother and father had apparently agreed that it would be bad for morale to cancel a party that had been a Quest staple for the last decade. The employees needed this boost with so many new worries surfacing over the last few months.

"It looks great." Robbie finished the champagne and placed the glass on a nearby table.

A chamber orchestra played in the foyer to welcome guests while a full band complete with a horn section blasted some forties standards in the living area. The furniture and carpets had been cleared away, the fireplaces turned into bar stations. There was a catering truck outside and most of the staff at the party had been supplied by the catering company. The set-up was similar to the other galas that had been held at the big house, but what made this year special was the decor.

In the past his mother had done themes around the horses or she'd turned the room into a Vegas-style casino, an English drawing room or an Indian rajah's palace. But this year, Jenna had carried over the harvest theme into the gala, importing an illuminated blue moon over the dance floor and lining the walls with small deciduous trees in a range of fall colors. Corn stalks filled in between, and sculptures made from brightly colored gourds decorated the cocktail tables that had been scattered around the rooms. A scarecrow sat in front of the band while lifelike blackbirds had been suspended from the ceiling, surprising an occasional dancer as they floated about the room on invisible strings.

"The decor is different." Robbie tugged at his tie.

"But I feel a little overdressed for the Haunted Hoedown or whatever theme Mom's got this year."

Melanie rolled her eyes.

"It's a Harvest Gala—no more and no less. Mom wanted to get back to a more simple party that connected us to the seasons without shoving the horses down everyone's throats."

"We've had the horses on our minds enough lately anyhow," Robbie said. Leopold's Legacy's racing days were on hold, with no possibility of the ban being lifted until his sire was identified. And no progress had been made there.

"Speaking of which, I wonder if you would mind talking to a reporter friend of mine who is doing some investigating on our behalf," Melanie said.

Robbie tensed.

"A reporter?"

"She's one of the good guys, Robbie. You remember Julia Nash? She gave us some good coverage back in June when the news first broke that Apollo's Ice wasn't Legacy's sire."

Melanie pointed out a woman examining the labels on two bottles of wine at the nearest bar station. Tall and elegant-looking, Julia Nash wore a classic navy cocktail dress that would have been in style ten years ago and would no doubt still be appropriate ten years into the future. She wore her hair in a simple style and Robbie guessed she was good at blending into the surroundings as though she belonged. And while she was definitely attractive, he found himself longing to see a dark-haired office manager with a taste for brighter colors and a hidden love of adventure beneath her reserved exterior.

And yeah, he still wanted to see her. Even after she'd all but booted him out the previous weekend after a round of kisses that had made his blood simmer.

"I'll talk to the reporter if you say she's cool." Robbie had grown closer to his sister in the past few months and he trusted her opinion on the woman.

"Great." Melanie grinned, her teeth flashing as she peered around the dance floor, which was starting to fill up. "Just try not to go off on any Robbie rants, okay?"

"I make no promises." He had every intention of being polite, but no man should have to suffer fools silently.

And no man could possibly keep his mind on this party when Amanda dominated his every thought.

"So do you think Amanda blew off the gala?" Melanie looked around the party again, her attention seeming to focus on Marcus Vasquez as the band started "Sentimental Reasons." "She's got a ready excuse since she has kids."

"I don't think she'd do that. I think she feels really indebted to Mom for hiring her."

Marcus looked their way and Robbie gave a terse nod for the sake of working relations. He didn't think Quest would be big enough for both of them for much longer, but he knew it would upset his sister if he talked about leaving. Besides, he didn't have any concrete plans—just a sense that he wouldn't be content staying on as Marcus's second in command.

"I don't know why Amanda thinks Mom did her any favors. Did you know she singlehandedly overhauled the office's computer files in less than three weeks? Now she's designing some kind of company Intranet to make the files more searchable and accessible." Melanie peered back over her shoulder to where Marcus had been and Robbie wondered if the man made her as uncomfortable as he did Robbie.

But Marcus had taken off with one of the horse owners who stabled his Thoroughbreds at Quest. That was the one part of the guy's job that Robbie didn't envy. There were plenty of owners starting to wonder if the negative publicity surrounding Quest Stables might affect their own horses. As head trainer, Marcus would have to generate some positive P.R. with Quest's clients.

"I didn't know about her work." Robbie hadn't asked Amanda much about her responsibilities and she hadn't shared anything with him.

Then again, Amanda was the kind of woman who put her family first, her conversation gravitating to the boys. Robbie liked that about her. He flagged down one of the servers in a white uniform with a pumpkin-colored pocket square that could have only come from Robbie's mother.

Ordering a double shot of bourbon, he wondered how much more time he needed to clock tonight before he could head home with a clear conscience.

"Have you given up on her already?" Melanie asked, surprising him.

"What do you mean?" He thought about timing the waitress with his bourbon.

If Melanie went down the road he thought she wanted to take, he was going to need the sustenance.

"Amanda." She stretched out the name to stress every syllable as if he'd been brain dead not to guess who she meant. "You aren't letting her off the hook that easily, are you?"

Robbie shook his head, having no clue how his sister could have any idea what was happening in his personal life.

"Contrary to popular belief, she was never on the hook. And I don't know what makes you think I'd ever coerce a woman into hanging out with me if she didn't want to stick around."

"I guess I'm just not used to seeing you take what life dishes out without a fight." She winked at him and squeezed his hand. "Good luck."

Before he could ask her what the hell she meant by that, she turned on her purple satin heel and disappeared into a throng of partygoers quickly filling up the room.

He swore under his breath just as the scent of vanilla tickled his nose.

"Hello, Robbie." Amanda appeared at his elbow, her fingers landing lightly on his forearm to claim his attention. "Do you have a minute? I'd like to talk to you."

For about two seconds, Robbie allowed himself to feel indignant about the way she'd called an end to things the previous weekend and the way he'd felt gut-shot all week without her.

But then he noticed the worry in her dark eyes and the pale circles underneath them that she couldn't quite cover with makeup. He couldn't deny this woman anything.

"As long as you promise we can go somewhere far removed from Hoedown Hell and the sound of forced laughter, I've got all the time in the world."

Chapter Ten

Amanda followed Robbie through the big house to a staircase leading away from the festivities. They passed a library and another veranda where more couples danced to the muted strains of a Spanish guitar. The patio heaters kept the cold at bay for the outdoor dancers, but Amanda had felt a chill in the air all week and was grateful to trail Robbie up the long staircase into the quieter, warmer portion of the house.

At the top of the steps he held open the door to a study, a room full of dark, rich woods and heavy paneled wainscoting. The walls were lined with scenes from the Kentucky Derby, both pen-and-ink drawings of the winners and framed photographs of various Prestons at Churchill Downs for the most exciting two minutes in sports. All the women wore hats and the men wore bow ties, the pictures almost a doorway to another era even though some of them were dated just last year.

This was Robbie's world.

The realization seeped in deeper than it had in the past, since she was accustomed to seeing him apart from his family, wearing his Quest Stables T-shirt and working with the horses. But tonight, more than ever, she saw beyond the horse trainer to the wealthy heir, a part of the vast Preston legacy.

"You look great," she told him, unable to come up with the right words to express how incredibly sexy and intimidating he seemed at the same time. Something about his classically cut tuxedo robbed her of speech. The temptation to lay her hand on his jacket, to splay her fingers across his strong chest, bit her hard.

"If you keep looking at me like that, I guarantee we're going to end up right back where every other private conversation takes us lately."

His voice took on a dark, intimate tone that shot a thrill clean through her.

"Where might that be?"

"Breathless and out of control." He took a step away from her and reached for a crystal decanter on a low bookshelf. "And since you've made it clear you're not going down that road with me, I think we'd better be careful."

He poured two glasses half full with a dark amber liquid and handed her one.

She took hers with a tentative sniff.

"Wow." The sharp sting of the alcohol burned her nasal passages while Robbie downed the contents of his glass. "What is it?"

"Maker's Mark—Kentucky bourbon." He replaced his glass on the tray and watched her as she raised hers to her lips.

Her mouth trembled under his gaze as the liquid flowed over her tongue. The bourbon tingled all the way down, the drink seeming to hit her bloodstream the moment she swallowed.

"So what did you want to talk about?" Robbie broke his gaze and turned to walk around the study. He spun a globe with one hand and then stopped it with the other.

"I want to apologize for the way things came to an abrupt halt last weekend." She tasted the sweet sting of the drink on her tongue as she set her glass on the nearby desk.

"You told me all along you weren't looking for a relationship so I wasn't surprised when you called off what was happening." He flicked on a desk lamp with a green glass shade and ran his finger over a brass paperweight bearing the Quest logo. "I've got no one to blame but myself for pushing you to consider something more between us."

The coolness in his tone hurt as much as his lack of focus on her, although she understood why he wanted to shut her out. He wasn't about to risk another rebuff and she didn't blame him.

"No." She moved closer to him but stopped short of touching him. She wasn't ready for a rebuff, either. "You didn't push me. Or—if you did—it was only a push that I needed to start moving on with my life."

He turned slowly and seemed to see her anew. A wrinkle appeared between his eyes as if he couldn't figure her out.

"What are you saying?"

She became aware of how close she'd been standing to him, her body mere inches from his in the warm privacy of the study. From downstairs she could hear the strains of the band playing "Moonglow" and the occasional bark of laughter, but the sounds seemed far away, apart from her world with Robbie.

"I'm saying that having you in my life has helped me wake up. I've been asleep to the world around me since my husband died—or at least asleep to everything but the boys. I wouldn't even have considered being with you unless you'd forced me to see what I'd be missing."

He shook his head and a sigh whistled between his teeth.

"I never wanted to force you into anything, though. Sometimes I can be so convinced I'm right that I can't see anyone else's point of view." He grinned. "I hope you know my sister would trade a whole lot of her blue ribbons to hear me say that."

"Well, whether you think it was right or wrong, I needed that forcefulness to help me see what I'm missing." She smoothed her fingers down the front of her red shawl, a long-ago gift from her mother. "I've been so certain I need to protect the boys from the pain of getting attached to boyfriends who might not stay in my life that I've ignored how much they might benefit from having someone around to admire their Lego forts now and then."

She'd thought that and a whole lot more in the last week since installing her security locks, realizing she would be walled up in an ivory tower if she didn't make some lifestyle changes soon.

"Not that I expect you—or anyone in my life—to jump right in and start playing dad to the boys." She didn't want to misrepresent her expectations, but she did want to be sure Robbie knew she was ready to make a few changes.

He went very still and Amanda half wished she still had that glass of bourbon in her hand so she could steal a bracing sip.

"So you've changed your mind? About…being with me?"

The atmosphere shifted, the air becoming thick with unspoken hungers. She still didn't know how to reconcile her old feelings for Dan with this new, sharp desire for Robbie. But she wouldn't let doubt rule her any longer.

"I don't know what kind of future I could promise, but I'm ready to—I don't know—pick up where we left off at my place last weekend."

"You were scared then," he reminded her, his sea-blue eyes never leaving hers. She could lose herself in their depths.

"I've been receiving hang-up calls and I got nervous about the boys being out of the house at the neighbor's."

Robbie frowned and she knew she couldn't wait to confide in him. She should have told him everything last weekend, but she'd been jittery and hadn't thought through the situation clearly. She'd been so focused on getting the boys back home and contacting Dan's old partner that she hadn't been fair to Robbie.

"Why would hang-up calls be threatening to your sons?"

She wrapped the shawl tighter around her shoulders, wishing she didn't come to this man with so many worries strapped on her back.

"I—need to have a seat." She lowered herself to the edge of the desk that was the central piece of furniture in the room. "My late husband was a police officer killed in the line of duty when he was shot by a drug dealer."

He sucked in a breath and took a step toward her, reaching out a comforting hand. "My God, Amanda, I had no idea—"

"We've come to a measure of acceptance about it, but during the drug bust, Dan shot a member of the gang before he was killed himself. The dead man's brother vowed revenge—or so I've been told by Dan's friends in the LAPD."

He took a seat on the edge of the desk right next to her and wound his arm around her waist.

That unspoken support soothed her conscience about dragging all her problems to his door. No matter what romantic dynamic might be at work between them, Robbie had become a friend. He cared that she might be in danger.

"Has this guy threatened you?" Robbie's muscles seemed to expand, his whole posture squaring up to an unseen enemy.

"There was an outburst at his trial—I didn't take it all that seriously at the time since he was on his way to jail. But he didn't receive much of a sentence and I started getting some late-night hang-up calls right before this guy got out of jail when we were still in L.A. I decided to get out of the state to be safe."

"But the calls are continuing?"

"There have only been a few of them, and I'd like to write them off as telemarketing gone awry, or maybe I inherited the phone number of someone whose friends are still calling and who then disconnect when they realize they've reached the wrong party." She tipped her head onto his shoulder for just a moment, taking strength from his nearness while the band downstairs played an old-fashioned waltz that created an unlikely musical score for her most frightening revelations.

"Your gut tells you otherwise." Robbie's chin settled on her hair as she leaned into him. A perfect fit.

If she closed her eyes to shut out the understated wealth of the room and the lifestyle difference that would make any relationship more awkward,

Amanda could almost pretend they were a couple. It felt good to share her worries and take comfort in Robbie's concern.

"I called the police and they've worked with the phone company to set up a system where we can find out who called the next time no one answers. I also put in some new locks and we've alerted the boys' school and Claudia at the after-care program to be extra vigilant."

He edged away from her enough to meet her gaze, his blue eyes warm with compassion.

"I'm so sorry you have to worry about this, Amanda, but you don't have to worry alone." He traced the outline of her jaw with his knuckle, rubbing a warm path to her chin.

"I appreciate you looking out for us." She knew the boys were safe with Claudia tonight since Claudia's son was a Marine home on leave for the next two weeks. Amanda had signed up for the boys to stay with Claudia during the gala along with the children who lived at Quest Stables. The caregiver had set up her house like a cinema for the occasion, with different movies playing in separate rooms according to age.

Still, even knowing the boys were safe for a few hours didn't take the edge off her fears. Having Robbie sit with her—sharing the anxiety—helped.

"It's not just me." He stroked her hair behind her ear then repeated the action. "We've got hundreds of people employed at Quest and they all would help you bear this burden if you let them."

Frowning, she wondered what he meant.

"I don't understand. There isn't anything more we can do. The police in California will let me know if this guy doesn't show up for his meetings with his probation officer. Until then, there's not much I can do besides be careful."

Robbie's jaw tightened.

"There is something else you can do. You can move in here."

Robbie didn't expect Amanda to agree right away.

She'd been dodging a relationship and in some ways he'd allowed her to because of his own misgivings. His professional life was a mess and he was starting to look beyond Quest—quietly—for other opportunities as a trainer. He couldn't afford to make a commitment to a woman who deserved better than a life spent traveling around for the sake of his rocky career. But his suggestion that she move onto Preston property wasn't about him.

"I don't understand." She straightened where she sat on the desk, her shawl falling off one shoulder until she tugged it back into place. "I can't move anywhere. I just spent all my savings relocating—"

"You wouldn't have to make this a permanent change so you wouldn't have to bring much with you." He could already see her here. Hell, she belonged here more than he did. "There are guest cabins open on the property that would be big enough for you and the boys. You could transplant a few things out here for a month or two until the cops figure out if this bastard is behind the dead calls."

He was ready to start packing her suitcases now.

For that matter, he wished she would move right in with him so he could watch over her personally, but he didn't think she'd go for that. And damn, but he couldn't believe how important it was to him that she was safe. The fierceness he felt in his chest at the first mention of some gang member who wanted revenge—he'd never experienced an emotion so raw.

"That's very kind of you to offer." She bit her full lip, her eyes darting around the room as if she was chasing down a thought. "I think it's actually a good idea. I just don't know about juggling a second rent."

"I'm not making a business proposition here." He ground his teeth, hoping she wouldn't be stubborn about something as important as her safety. "I'm extending hospitality to a friend. There's no rent involved. I know my mom would have already made the offer if she knew about the problem."

Amanda crossed her ankles, making him aware of the red flip-flops she wore under a long white gown with red roses stitched along the waist and the neck. He smiled at the hints of her more casual surfer girl ways beneath the sophisticated clothes she liked to wear. The memory of her in her blue duckling pajamas flashed through his brain, unleashing another tide of hunger for her.

"I—" She shook her head, her short, dark hair slipping from the tiny rhinestone flower that held it off her face. "It seems like I'd be imposing and I probably shouldn't accept, but how can I say no when it might keep the boys safe?"

Relief flowed through his veins and he pulled her to him. Squeezed her.

"I can drive you over to your place now so you can retrieve some things before you have to pick up the boys." He couldn't let her go. Now that he knew she was in danger, he regretted the need to hold back all the more.

His brother Brent had lost his wife and it had nearly destroyed him, so Robbie had an idea how painful it must be for Amanda to lose her husband. He would never want to add to that hurt, but he also couldn't help the sense that holding back was robbing them both of an experience they'd never forget.

And, possibly, an experience that might help her to heal.

"That would be great," Amanda said finally, her words muffled against his tuxedo jacket.

He needed to let go, but it wasn't going to be easy. And this was just prying himself away from her after a hug. How would he find the restraint to leave her if they took the plunge she hinted she was ready to make? He might never be able to locate a place of his own where he could be the head trainer because if he got involved with this amazing woman, chances were good he'd never want to leave. He'd already contacted another horse farm with a head trainer opening.

"Robbie?" Amanda pulled away first, her hands remaining on his lapels, her fingers smoothing the silk.

"I'm grateful for the help and I'd be glad to hide away for a while. It will look like I'm living in Twisted River while I'm secretly living here. I won't even put in a phone line. I'll just use my cell and keep the phones connected at the condo."

"Good." He liked this plan, and now that they'd agreed on it, he wanted to put it in action. "If we hurry we can make it to Twisted River and back to pick up your things before the hoedown ends."

Amanda smiled and he realized he didn't see that very often when she wasn't with the kids. The woman had too many worries on her mind.

"Hoedown?" She slid off the desk, her flip-flops hitting the floor with a slap. "I don't think that's quite what Jenna was going for."

"We rarely get what we bargain for in life, do we?" He gripped her hand in his, knowing they'd made a kind of commitment to each other tonight, even if the words hadn't been spoken aloud. And while he had no doubt he could provide extra protection for Amanda and the boys, he just hoped he'd be able to spend more time with her without hurting her in the long run.

She'd been through enough without him adding to the mix.

Still, he felt guilty for chasing her smile away so fast.

"You're damn right about that." She lifted an eyebrow and tilted her head to one side. "And I know this isn't exactly the kind of invitation you've been looking for from me, but would you like to come back to my place?"

Chapter Eleven

Sliding into the leather seat of Robbie's low-slung BMW was a far cry from vaulting onto the worn, juice-stained upholstery of her car, which was usually covered with popcorn kernels and microscopic-sized pieces of the boys' building sets.

Amanda had been so immersed in single-parenthood for the last two years—throwing herself into making up for Dan's absence from her sons' lives—that she'd made no time for herself. No time to be a grown-up.

She felt like a grown-up now. She'd invited Robbie into her life, if only for a little while. As a mother, she wouldn't have many opportunities to indulge her own wants and she couldn't deny she wanted Robbie.

With the night sky spread out across the horizon and the dark shape of rolling Kentucky hills in front of them, Amanda wanted to drive all night. Wanted themselves to propel straight into the stars with the scent of expensive leather and musky aftershave wafting about her nose, the hum of a sleekly built German engine purring beneath her feet, and a warm, vital man shifting into gear beside her.

"Thank you."

The sentiment wasn't just a response to a ride out to Twisted River to pick up her things. Because, while she was grateful to him for driving her to the condo and helping her with some suitcases, she was even more grateful for this chance to sit in the passenger seat for a little while—literally and figuratively. She'd been making so many big decisions on her own lately that it felt good to draw on his strength, if only for a short time.

"It's no problem," he assured her, assuming she was grateful for the ride. "I put in the required appearance at the gala and helped out at the festival today. My mom can't say I didn't participate." He glanced her way as he pulled out onto the interstate heading south. "You never came over to the pony rides today. I thought for sure I'd get to talk to you when you brought Max over."

"I was a little afraid that Kiefer would start giving broad hints about us dating and make things even more awkward before I had a chance to speak to you privately and apologize for last weekend." She could feel the Kentucky bourbon in her veins, just enough to heighten her rush when Robbie rounded a turn and picked up speed.

"You haven't learned how to shut down the match-maker impulse yet?" He glanced at her over the console, his teeth a flash of white in the dark.

Her whole body responded to that visual, her skin remembering the way those perfect pearly whites felt grazing lightly across her skin when he kissed her. Nipped her.

"Um…" She cleared her throat and wished she could dislodge her runaway imagination as easily. "I guess not because Kief still works that angle with me every chance he gets."

He downshifted for a stop sign and the edge of his hand grazed her calf. Heat burned her skin where his hand had been, no matter how briefly.

"You just have to needle him about the girls at school. Nothing puts a little matchmaking effort on hold like turning the tables."

Amanda's eyes lingered on Robbie's hand on the gearshift, his long fingers wrapped around the stick while a red-and-white lanyard fell forward around his wrist. Since she hadn't seen it before, she figured it must have been hidden under his shirt cuff. Probably a craft made by one of the kids at the gala.

"And you think that would work with Kiefer? He seems a little young to care one way or another about a conversation involving girls." She fought the temp-tation to cover his hand with hers, to slide her fingers between each of his.

"I know for a fact it works with Kiefer since I've tried it. I tease him about my nieces since the two of them love to flirt with your son. Kid stuff, you know? But the mere mention of the girls and Kiefer changes the subject in no time. Right after he turns pinker than dogwood in spring."

Amanda smiled along with him, glad to think Robbie had developed his own relationship with Kiefer apart from her. And while that was good news, it made her heart ache at the same time. Kiefer shared something different with Robbie—a relationship that a boy could find only with a male. She was grateful he'd found it and sad she hadn't been able to provide that for him these last two years.

"You've been really good to Kiefer," she observed lightly, trying hard to stay on top of her emotions tonight when she felt so sensitive. So raw.

"I don't know if he'd agree with you when I'm ribbing him about Katie and Rhea, but I hope you don't think I've been hanging out with your boy just to score points with his hot mother." He lifted his hand from the gearshift to rest on Amanda's leg. "He's a great kid in his own right."

Amanda murmured her agreement, her capacity for words stolen by Robbie's hand on her thigh just above her knee. She felt like a teenager at her first movie with a boy, aware of every subtle move of Robbie's hand, thrilling to every nuance of his touch through her silky dress.

"Here we are," he announced a few minutes later,

driving through the security gate and saving her from the potential embarrassment of taking his hand in hers and guiding it to all the places on her body that cried out for his touch.

She blinked to regain her focus and found herself in the parking lot outside her condo. Her lights were off except for the outdoor lantern near the front walk.

Time to remember why she'd come here. And it didn't have anything to do with Robbie Preston's hand on her thigh.

"Okay." She straightened in her seat and pressed a hand to the small square of skin exposed at her chest. Her flesh was warm. Probably as pink as Robbie had accused Kiefer of being when the subject of girls came up.

She didn't wait for Robbie to open her door once the car was parked since she needed a little fresh air to gather her wits. Restless and wound up, she dug in her purse for a key to the door and let Robbie steer her up the walk, his hand on her waist.

She'd told him she was ready for more between them, but her admission had gotten lost back in the study when she'd revealed her problems with Benny Orway. Had Robbie even caught her offer to explore the heat between them? She didn't know, and the mixture of anticipation and uncertainty made her heart trip too fast in her chest.

"Would you let me go in first?" He held out his hand for the key and she remembered the way Dan had needed to clear a room before she entered—a habit he'd learned early on growing up in rough neighborhoods.

Would the danger she might have brought to Kentucky spoil some of the peace Robbie found in his life here? Would her problems transform him into a man who needed to check out every room before she entered? God, she prayed not.

Nodding, she handed him the key and was grateful for his presence even as she regretted the need to draw him deeper into her life.

He let them inside and flicked on lights all over the condo, making a quick turn about the place while she set her shawl and purse on the kitchen island separating the cooking area from the family room.

"Can I help?" he offered, staring at her in the bright lights. "I can carry suitcases or—" he looked around the condo "—pack some dinosaurs?"

"Actually, I bought a timer for the outdoor lights last week." She hunted around a kitchen drawer and found the device still in the plastic wrap. "I could use it on a couple of living-room lights if you wouldn't mind setting it up while I put together some of the boys' things?"

They worked in synchronized silence for the next ten minutes, and when Amanda emerged from her bedroom in a simple, violet-colored shirt dress, pulling a suitcase on wheels behind her, she found Robbie methodically checking the lock on every window while he went around lowering all the blinds.

When he heard her he turned, and she couldn't

help a rush of feminine pleasure as his eyes traveled over her. The perusal was brief but definite, a universal male compliment.

"You changed," he observed lightly, releasing the cord to the blinds on a window near the fireplace.

"You don't like it?" she asked, only because she was confident he did.

She'd had an unsteady day—an uneasy month. For that matter, it had been a rip-roaring bad few years. So what if she fished for some attention from a gorgeous, caring, one-of-a-kind man—she figured she darn well deserved a break.

"You look hot," he admitted, his eyes turning a darker shade of blue as he took a step closer. And then another. "It's just that I envy you the freedom of comfortable clothes while I'm still in a penguin suit."

"Feel free to take it off." She didn't know quite where such bold words came from, but she couldn't make herself regret the suggestion.

Especially not when Robbie's gaze went from dark to downright feral.

"Don't tempt me, lady, when we've got time constraints." He held himself rigid a few feet away.

And then—despite all good sense—her body temperature spiked. Her belly tightened with carnal hunger, her thighs twitching restlessly beneath her skirt.

"It's probably not the right time," she agreed, hating that she'd wasted time denying the inevitable where this man was concerned.

She'd reached the point that she wouldn't forgive

herself if she didn't follow this attraction to see where it led, and now that she'd made up her mind to move forward, she couldn't seem to fulfill the desire fast enough.

Robbie glanced up at the clock on the kitchen wall. Then he settled his attention on her again.

"How late can we pick up the boys?"

She double-checked her watch while her pulse leaped.

"Forty minutes."

His eyes narrowed, his whole body tensing.

"I've pushed you before and you wouldn't even consider getting close to me."

She could feel the possibility of intimacy in the air and it made her lightheaded. The chaos of scattered toys at her feet faded away as her focus narrowed to this moment. This man. She'd been closed to any kind of sensual feeling for so long and now all those suppressed urges came roaring to the surface, demanding to be acknowledged. Fulfilled.

And, oh, my, she had the feeling Robbie Preston would fulfill them more deliciously than she could ever imagine.

"At first I didn't want to unload all the problems from my past with you or anyone at Quest, and I was resistant to getting involved with someone the boys might get attached to prematurely." She licked her lips, knowing those reservations still applied to a smaller degree. "But I can't fight it anymore. It hurts to see you and not to be able to—touch you."

He moved toward her so quickly she didn't have time to think. React. He locked his arms around her and pressed the length of his body against her.

Yes.

Every cell in her body seemed to leap in response, and if his arms hadn't been holding her up she would have collapsed or possibly melted at his feet.

His hands roamed over her back and sank lower. Lower. She arched into him, taking everything he offered her and asking for more. He'd been in her dreams too many nights for her to waste this precious time with him now. "I've wanted you to touch me ever since the cocktail party at your mother's," she confessed, defending her reason for flying into his arms.

She attempted to pull off his tuxedo jacket, but when her efforts proved futile, he helped her, easing it the rest of the way off his arms while she tugged loose his tie and undid his shirt buttons.

"I've wanted to touch you since I first saw you." He kissed her mouth and licked a path around the rim of her lower lip.

The slow slide of his tongue made her senses hum.

"That day with Kiefer out in the paddock?" She couldn't imagine him wanting her when she hadn't even been all that polite, afraid Kiefer was bothering the boss.

"No. I saw you before that." He unfastened the belt on her shirt dress and the purple fabric gaped open. "Outside the stable offices. You were talking to Marcus."

The fierce note in his voice assured her he didn't approve of the choice of company. He ran a finger down the center of her chest, starting at her neck and easing down to the valley between her breasts. She shivered in response, intrigued that he'd seen her before she'd ever laid eyes on him.

"Did you think I was your rival's lover?"

"I thought you had pretty eyes." He flicked the silk off her shoulders and the dress pooled at her feet in a soft *swish.* "I wanted to see how they would look if I did this."

He brought her hips to his and positioned her core over the ridge of his erection. Even through the layer of her satin panties and the silk of his trousers, the heat of him twisted her insides with a sharp, sensual ache. He stared down into her eyes, his expression hard and hot. Unreadable except for the desire for her.

"Please," she whispered, her need too great for her to be subtle. "Touch me."

Robbie didn't have to be told twice.

He'd passed the point of no return when he took Amanda's dress off and got an eyefull of her curves in violet lace panties. Any reservations faded the moment he knew she'd gone into that bedroom of hers and changed for him.

And there was no question this satin and lace underwear was intended for a man's eyes. The bra pulled her breasts high and only just barely covered her. With tiny bows sewn down the straps and across the front, the garment was made to be seen.

He lowered his mouth to her cleavage, savoring the vanilla scent that rose from a hidden spot between her breasts. Another time he would savor every delectable inch of her, but right now he needed to have her stretched out underneath him, her sleek feminine heat surrounding him. Lowering her to the couch, he left her just long enough to shed the rest of his clothes and retrieve a condom from his wallet. He'd carried one ever since the U of L football game, hoping they'd be at this point one day.

She reached to stroke him before he rolled on the protection and he nearly lost it. His past relationships had never had this kind of effect on him, his release already gathering low in his shaft. She peered up at him through half-lowered lids, her eyes glassy with the same hunger that rode him.

He tugged her panties down her thighs, unable to wait any longer.

The world disappeared. A metal toy car between the couch cushions tore into his knuckles but it didn't bother him as he positioned himself between her thighs.

"Look at me." He palmed her cheek and waited for her eyes to meet his, needing her to see him, to acknowledge the rightness of being with him. "See how much I want this. You."

She made a little sound of agreement in her throat, the noise a soft purr of want. He answered it by easing inside her.

Hunger for full possession swamped him, and he had all he could do to move slowly. She arched her back underneath him, trying to help, encouraging him with a soft, sexy roll of her hips. Still, it had been a long time for her and he didn't want to rush it.

But then she lifted her legs to wrap around his and he was powerless against the hot clamp of her feminine muscles around his shaft. His toes pressed tight to the arm of the sofa as he leveraged himself deeper inside her.

So. Damn. Good.

Her eyes held his, just as he'd asked. But he hadn't anticipated how deeply affected he'd be at the feel of her giving herself to him completely. The connection was deep and binding, and it scared the hell out of him even as he was powerless to look away.

He pumped his hips in a slow rhythm, gaining momentum as his heart rate kicked up and his body demanded more. Hotter. Deeper.

The flush on Amanda's skin heated him. He felt the tremors along her thighs that told him she was close to her peak. Reaching between her legs he found the hot core of her and plucked the taut flesh with his thumb and forefinger until her whole body stiffened. Arched. Convulsed in sweet fulfillment.

With another drive of his hips, he allowed himself to feel every lush contraction around his flesh. The physical proof that she'd found completion in his arms brought him to the edge faster than any touch.

He hurtled into bliss right behind her, his shout a hoarse cry that filled the room.

He slumped over her in the aftermath, his arms still keeping his weight off her while she stroked his back in the darkness. He wanted to lie with her for days and not move except to touch her. Make love to her.

But he knew they needed to leave. Reality called them to get back to Quest to pick up her boys. And, as much as he hated to go, throwing themselves into setting her up in a staff cabin at Quest would provide a distraction to keep them from overanalyzing what had just happened here.

Because as far as Robbie was concerned, the night had been about more than first-time intimacy. Something deep and elemental had passed between them and he wasn't sure he was ready to explore that any more than Amanda would be.

Chapter Twelve

She'd slept with another man. A man who wasn't her husband.

Amanda didn't know how she should be feeling about that as she stared up at the ceiling long after midnight. Robbie had contacted his mother to explain his concerns for Amanda's safety and Jenna had assigned her and the boys a cabin for the next month. Robbie helped her locate the small building, then he'd carried in the suitcases and dutifully exclaimed over an art project Max had worked on while at Claudia's house—a painting of Kiefer on a purple and black horse. And then he was gone, slipping out while Amanda put the kids to bed, perhaps so his presence wouldn't seem awkward.

That had been thoughtful of him, since bedtime was one of those special, family-only times. Still, she'd missed him after he left. She missed him now, long after the kids had been tucked in, as she stared up at the rough-hewn rafters of the cabin. Besides two bedrooms, a family room, kitchen and laundry area, the cabin had a small upstairs terrace off her bedroom, a perfect spot to watch the stars.

Or peer into Robbie's bedroom a mere acre away across a patch of open meadow. She could see his cabin from the terrace, a bonus he'd pointed out to her before he left. Surely he just meant to make her feel safe—and it did. But the revelation also had her wondering if she'd be tempted to play voyeur sometime.

But mostly Amanda thought about how truly generous it had been of the Prestons to accommodate her here. She felt safer already.

Kevin had called her earlier in the week to say Benny Orway had showed up for his last meeting with his probation officer, so between that bit of reassurance and the temporary relocation to Quest Stables while police investigated the aborted calls, Amanda felt better. In fact, the only thing that made her feel uneasy tonight was the fact that she'd given herself without reservation to another man.

"Dan's gone," she whispered to herself, trying to reconcile the moments of guilt with the sweet ache of her thighs from lovemaking earlier.

And perhaps she wouldn't have felt so disloyal to Dan if her time with Robbie hadn't been so mind-numbingly fantastic. Her whole body warmed to think about the way he'd touched her.

Her cell phone vibrated on the top of Amanda's suitcase, dancing around in a circle on the makeshift nightstand. Her stomach tensed. Had Orway found her cell number? But as she flipped open the phone, she saw a familiar name.

"You left without saying goodbye," she accused in a soft whisper, her mouth curving into a smile that Robbie would call her here. Now. When she'd just been thinking about him.

"I didn't want to put too much pressure on you if you were feeling…awkward about where things stood between us."

His voice sounded low and husky. Sexy and sleep-ready.

"Are you sure you weren't trying to run for the hills after spending ten minutes in the house with two rambunctious, overtired boys determined to out-shout one another?" The kids hadn't been badly behaved. Just noisy and eager to outdo each other in front of an audience.

"I told you I've got a soft spot in my heart for rowdy kids. I was shushed and elbowed into silence a lot so it's sort of fun to encourage your kids to let loose."

"Hey, no working out your childhood issues with my kids if it involves making them even louder than normal." She couldn't imagine Jenna being the kind of parent to silence her children, but Amanda hadn't gotten a good read on Robbie's father, Thomas.

Thomas seemed quieter, but she wouldn't have pegged him for a harsh parent. Still, even the most well-meaning fathers could have high expectations for their sons.

"Did they get to sleep okay in the new place?"

She heard a sound in the background that might have been the rustling of bed sheets. Then again, maybe she just wanted an excuse to visualize him under the covers.

"Yes. Max was already falling asleep at the sink while he brushed his teeth, so he was snoring ten seconds after I tucked him in. But even Kiefer settled down pretty quickly. He really likes it here since you taught him how to ride." She'd been wrong to push Robbie away with both hands when he'd already brought good things into their lives. Maybe she'd just been making excuses not to get close to a man again.

Then again, what if she got too close—and the kids got too close—to a man who didn't have family aspirations?

"Amanda?" Robbie's sheets rustled again. "I know you don't want to create a lot of false expectations for the boys if we get involved. So I was thinking it might benefit all of us if you and I...tested the waters on neutral ground."

Her grip on the phone tightened and she jacked herself out of bed, her nerves jittering at the suggestion.

"What do you mean?" Rising from the warmth of her blankets, she wrapped her arms around herself and strode closer to the door leading out to the deck.

The lights were off in Robbie's cabin so he must be talking to her in the dark.

"Come outside." His voice hitched on the soft command.

"Can you see me?" She turned to look behind her even though she knew there were no lights on to illuminate her in the glass door overlooking the upstairs terrace.

"The moon is full and it caught a hint of your nightgown. I can't see you well, but I'm sitting outside and I can just tell that you're there. Looking this way."

Her heart thudded in her chest as she stepped outside into the chilly night. Fall was making the nights colder as September progressed. Her breath huffed out in a visible puff as she looked up at the stars above her.

Her gaze shifted down to Robbie's terrace and she glimpsed his rangy body sprawled out over a lounge. He had one foot propped on the railing.

"Hi. So what do you have in mind?" She leaned her elbows on her own rail and stared out into the night, the air rushing over her face.

Everything appeared quiet.

"I thought we could take a day away from Quest to go to the races and—I don't know. Have a real date. Maybe spend the night in Lexington afterward."

Heat bloomed inside her.

"So we'd be sort of dating in secret?"

"It would take some of the pressure off you so you wouldn't have to worry about the boys getting the wrong impression of us being together. And I know my mom is already asking me when we'll be coming up to the house for Friday-night cocktails together, so—"

"You're feeling the pressure, too." Amanda couldn't help but take a small amount of pleasure from Robbie's admission. She was glad Jenna didn't mind them dating.

Unless he'd only told her half the story.

"Do you think your family would be against us seeing each other?"

"Tonight when I called my mother to ask about a cabin, she warned me not to hurt you. But I don't know why she'd automatically think—"

"You wouldn't hurt me. At least, you would never try to." Amanda was touched that Jenna would look out for her, even if she couldn't help a twinge of indignation on Robbie's behalf.

"So, what do you think, pretty lady?" Robbie's voice teased her senses in the dark, his tempting offer still on the table. "Would you consider ditching work one day this week to go to the track and let me show you the racing world through a trainer's eyes? You deserve the extra time off after working weekends."

She could probably ask Claudia to keep the boys overnight. As long as Claudia's son was still home with her, she would feel as safe—if not safer— having the boys under their roof. Having a Marine in the bedroom next to Kiefer and Max gave Amanda reassurance.

"It depends. I'd like to see a whole lot more than

the race track." She shouldn't flirt with him so shamelessly when this attraction between them probably wouldn't last. Would she look back on this time and cringe at how she'd practically thrown herself at a hot younger man? A man so far out of her league it was probably delusional of her to date him in the first place?

Still, one more night with him wouldn't pose a risk to her heart. Not when she had the weight of the world on her shoulders with Orway's threat.

"You'll get everything you ask for and more," he promised, and she could see him push up out of the lounge chair on his terrace to prowl the space with a restless gait. "Is that a yes?"

She wanted to say yes as badly as she wanted to race across that acre and tackle him into a real bed. But she had too many responsibilities simply to follow her desires the way she had in her days as a surfer girl, living for the next good wave.

"Just as long as we understand each other." She turned away from the view of his cabin, needing to think with her head and not her heart. She knew Robbie was a good man and that she was ready to let him into her life—but she would take it slowly to protect the boys. And, maybe, to protect herself, too. "We'll just take this one day at a time, right? I don't want to rush headlong into something one of us might regret."

She knew who the "one of us" might be, and—call her a coward—she was still scared that Robbie would turn around one day and wonder why he'd trapped himself into a relationship with an older woman and a ready-made family.

Robbie was silent for so long she peered back across the meadow before she shut the door.

"If one day at a time is all I can get from you, then I'll take it."

Amanda swallowed past the lump that had formed in her throat, knowing she'd done the right thing even if her heart cried out for more. But she would savor every stolen second with him before he changed his mind. Before she was forced to get back to her old life.

A life that couldn't include an enticing and impulsive man who brought out the wild and reckless woman inside her who she thought she'd buried a long time ago.

Chapter Thirteen

Churchill Downs might have been the most famous racetrack in Kentucky, but it wasn't the prettiest. It looked good enough in the Derby Day footage that was watched across more TV screens in American households than any other Thoroughbred race, but up close the legendary Louisville track was low on charm and high on professional bettors smoking cigars and studying their racing forms as if the papers held the clues to the universe.

So Robbie took Amanda to Keeneland for her introduction to the Thoroughbred world through his eyes, an effort that might be wasted on a woman who had made it clear she wanted to move slowly. Which would probably be for the best since he'd lined up an interview for a trainer position at a facility in Texas next week. He probably wasn't in a position to get involved any more than Amanda was, but that didn't stop him from regretting their lack of time together. Her one-day-at-a-time approach didn't exactly make him hopeful for a future together.

"It's beautiful," Amanda observed, a wistful note in her voice as they walked past a row of painted cast-iron statues of jockeys. "And not at all what I envisioned."

They'd left the grandstand to explore the grounds and Robbie enjoyed steering her through the paths of vendors selling everything from corn dogs to original artwork of horses who'd become part of Keeneland history.

"There are a few tracks that really develop the park-like atmosphere and sense of racing history. Keeneland is one. Saratoga in upstate New York is another. They are smaller venues, but racing fans love them."

She paused to run an idle finger over a green lamppost with the signature golden *K* encircled by a wreath of flowers. All around them, hard-core gamblers in simple khakis and polo shirts mingled with fans who dressed up for the races. While the women here didn't wear the hats that were famous around the Kentucky Derby or at Ascot, there were still plenty of dresses with jackets and heels. Men sported suits and took care of business on cell phones outside the grandstand before returning to their seats with cold beers in plastic cups.

"If you had horses in a race today, where would you be?" Amanda asked. "Out here in the seats or wherever they keep the horses?" She peered around as if to solve the mystery of where the horses were kept.

She looked amazing in a fitted brown dress with a wide, square neck that was sexy without being overt. The jacket she wore over it had thin, feminine lapels that highlighted the neckline on the dress before coming together over a single button at her waist. A golden necklace glimmered in the fall sun, a delicately fashioned peace sign that made him smile.

They'd packed for an overnight trip to the Kentucky River Palisades. He'd booked a cabin for them and planned to show her the sights, but he didn't feel he could simply take her there the moment they stepped off Quest property. The race was a good way to spend at least a couple of hours before they found a little more privacy.

"The horses are quartered on the other side of the backstretch—" he pointed in the general direction "—but they're walked out in a paddock before each race so bettors can see the animals to make any last-minute decisions based on how the horse looks. I would usually be sprinting between the paddock, the grandstand and the stables, unable to sit still."

Even now he was antsy and he didn't have a horse running today.

"You get nervous when you have horses on the track?"

He stopped to consider, certain no one had asked him that question before.

"Not nervous. Excited, I guess." He steered her past a crowd gathered around a guitar player banging out an old folk song on the lawn behind the grandstand.

"Excited." He eyed the line of two-year-olds moving out into the paddock now and thought Something to Talk About could take any of them even with his late birthday. "My mother likes to say I was practically born trackside since she went into labor during the Bluegrass Stakes. And whether or not that has anything to do with it, I've always loved coming here—to any racetrack—to match the fruits of our labors against the competition."

Amanda paused to watch a painter fill in some background details on a canvas depicting the paddock area. The work was still in the rough stages, but Robbie recognized the guy as one of the Keeneland regulars.

"You're competitive." She seemed to weigh the idea as if it was all new to her. "I guess that makes sense as the youngest of three brothers."

Robbie didn't think she was making any big-time effort to get into his head, yet he wondered if maybe he'd purposely pitted himself against Andrew and Brent in the past. He'd always thought he had to prove himself, but maybe he'd occasionally pushed sibling rivalry too far. He didn't really need to break his nose so many times to become a flawless cliff diver before Brent tried the sport.

"I think my grandfather brought me here the most when I was young." Robbie had liked that Granddad had taken the time to do things just with him. "He was more committed to retirement by the time I was born so we'd come here every day during the spring and fall meets to check over the competition's horses."

He couldn't help but think Amanda's boys would love exploring every facet of the racetrack as much as he had as a kid. The image of him showing Kiefer and Max around felt so right it spooked him. He'd been so worried about hurting the kids if he got too close too fast and then things didn't work out with Amanda that he hadn't stopped to consider how saying goodbye to them might kick him in the gut.

"Is that what made you want to be a trainer?"

He led her to the paddock area, where they watched the horses walk the paved circle behind a split-rail fence.

"Yes and no. Granddad gave me a love of the behind-the-scenes preparation for race day since we spent a lot of time talking to the trainers and exercise riders to see which horses looked best. I'd never want to be in Andrew's shoes on the business side, even if he gets the most glory as the front man for Quest." Robbie noticed one of the two-year-olds looked edgy and nervous, her dark eyes unfocused as she tried to take in the surroundings.

Would Something to Talk About be that way in his first race? Melanie was entering the colt in a local race today that wasn't just for Thoroughbreds and therefore not affected by the racing commissions' sanctions against majority-owned Quest horses. It had been tough to let his horse run without him being there, but he knew the race was a good opportunity for the colt to prove himself to Marcus, and Robbie wouldn't break plans with Amanda. Not when he'd be leaving for Texas—at least temporarily.

"And what made you choose to be a trainer specifically?" Amanda's eye went to a young mother pushing a stroller and he saw her wink at the toddler eating an ice cream cone.

All at once he regretted not getting to see Amanda with her kids when they were younger. A foolish wish since the kids belonged to another man, and if Robbie had been around her then he would have had to ignore any attraction to her.

"Do you want the totally honest answer or the one I normally give out?" He hated to share his real reason with her.

"Do you have to ask?" She smiled up at him, her dark eyes playful.

And just like that he wondered how much longer he'd have to extend their time here until he could take her back to the cabin he'd rented on a lake nearby.

"My father always said training a horse to race was the hardest part of this business."

She slipped her hand around his forearm, which rested on the top rail of the paddock fence. The feel of her hand on him made him think about the cabin he'd booked—the place where they could be alone and explore those touches to their incredible conclusion.

"And you couldn't resist proving you could take on the job that was toughest in his eyes."

"That about sums it up." He nodded as he waved to another trainer who'd taught him a lot about the business after college. "Doesn't say much for my family dynamics, does it?"

"I think it sounds totally normal to want a parent's approval. You just took the hard road to acceptance."

"Apparently, I'm still on it," he observed wryly, liking the way her fingers flexed against him, her nails raking lightly against the fabric of his shirt to tease the skin beneath.

The touch was simple. Almost innocent. Except the knowing light in her eyes told him she'd been having thoughts similar to his about that cabin....

The horses filed out of the paddock to make their way toward the racetrack as post time approached. The crowd waited for them to clear the walkway before making their way to the betting booths or finding their seats.

He wrapped his arm around Amanda's waist, thinking how perfectly she fit against him.

"I think you're going to prove a lot to your family once Something to Talk About wins his race today." She slipped her arm beneath his jacket, her fingers resting just above his hipbone.

And wasn't it almost time to peel out of the parking lot and take her somewhere private?

"How did you know about that race?" He'd kept it quiet around the stables on purpose, not needing any extra pressure for a performance that meant a lot to him personally and professionally. He would have attended it himself except that Melanie thought she might turn in the best performance if she felt more low key about the day. He definitely didn't want to make her tense.

"Melanie had me file the paperwork to enter him," she admitted. "Your sister asked me to keep it on the down-low and I've got to say she's a persuasive person."

"She's a pistol." Robbie guided Amanda through the grandstand and out to the rail so they could see this race up close. "Any woman who wants to make it as a jockey has to be tough and determined, but Melanie charms people so fast they don't always realize how strong she is."

"My husband was like that." Her brow furrowed as if she picked apart an old memory. "He sort of reeled you in before you had a chance to think. People were drawn to him, and if he wanted you in his life, you couldn't possibly say no."

Amanda stretched up on her toes to see over the crowd already gathering at the rail and Robbie pointed out a spot close to the finish line that was still vacant, humbled that she would share a memory of this man he sometimes feared he couldn't live up to.

"And he drew you in, too?" He wanted to tread carefully here, but he sensed something troubling in her voice.

Could the husband that she'd mourned all this time have hurt her?

"Yes. Dan was always fun to be around, but he was strong-willed and he could be tough to argue with if you didn't agree with him." The furrow in her brow cleared as she abruptly changed the subject. "But what about Something to Talk About? Why the secrecy about the race?"

Amanda settled in next to an older couple recording every second of their track experience on a digital camcorder. He would honor her obvious wish not to discuss her husband anymore, preferring to let her spin out the details at her own speed. Still, he wondered if there had been problems in Amanda's marriage before her husband died, and maybe just a small selfish part of him was grateful his personality was different from Dan's.

No one would ever accuse Robbie of being especially social, or having the kind of dynamic personality people flocked to be around. The lone-wolf gig suited him just fine.

Or rather it had until he realized how much he enjoyed sharing this day with Amanda.

The trumpeter came out to sound the call for post time as the horses made their way into the starting gate. All around them, racegoers compared notes about track conditions and their predictions for the next winner.

"I don't need the extra scrutiny on me right now and I'm just superstitious enough that I wouldn't want Marcus betting against me." He edged closer to Amanda as the crowd thickened behind him. "I'm hoping to run Something to Talk About in the Sandstone Derby in Dubai since the ban only keeps Quest horses from Thoroughbred racing in North American competitions."

The gentle brush of her body against his made him vow this would be the only race they'd watch today. If his time with Amanda was going to be limited to one day at a time, he'd damn well make the most of it.

"So you get around the ban by racing abroad or by racing here in meets that don't limit the field to Thoroughbreds." She peered up at him over one shoulder while the horn sounded for post time.

The horn blower in the green coat with gold braid was a Keeneland institution.

"Exactly."

"Who would you pick in this race?" she asked him at the last minute before the starting gate opened.

"The number-four horse. He's got a new trainer, but he looks great and the guy who's working with him is supposed to be talented. Hungry for victory."

"Like you."

He could hear the smile in her voice just as the horses broke free of the gate and he savored the sense of friendship in that moment as much as his attraction to her. Maybe it was because she'd lived a little longer than he had, but she looked at the world in a much more easygoing and insightful way. She seemed to understand him in a way no one else ever had and—incredibly—she liked what she saw. She didn't see a hothead or someone who was always second-best.

She saw something a hell of a lot better.

And as they watched the number-four horse easily push to the head of the pack just as he'd predicted, Robbie regretted his need to move on from Quest Stables, since Amanda Emory was proving to be everything he'd ever wanted in a woman. Tonight he would work his ass off to make her see the potential of a future with him. And as for the interview he'd arranged at that rival horse farm in Texas, he'd worry about that later. Because spending the day with her was only making him realize they shared something too good to walk away from without a fight.

Amanda recognized the feeling washing over her as surely as the September sunshine later that afternoon. She sat in the bow of a rowboat Robbie oared easily through a section of the Kentucky River called the Palisades, her eyes going to his rippling biceps more often than to the leaves just beginning to change color on the high limestone cliffs around them.

She felt pure, undiluted happiness.

That was a feeling she hadn't experienced in a long time, but she would never mistake it. She heard it in the rhythmic splash of the oars through the water and tasted it in the spicy red wine Robbie had packed for a picnic. Sure, she'd found joy in her children and some good times with friends who'd sought to distract her from the rut her life had fallen into after Dan died. But that hadn't been the same as the happiness she felt now, which seemed to soak through her skin and penetrate bone-deep.

Her boys had given her hugs and kisses goodbye this morning and they'd seemed as excited for her to take a trip as she was to have one. Of course, she hadn't told them she'd be staying with Robbie. Still, the memory of her kids happy at home mingled with her pleasure in being here and feeling deliciously like a grown-up across from this sexy, warm-hearted man…. The mood was so enticing, she didn't know how she would honor her dictate that they take it slow with a relationship.

"Can I ask you a question?" Robbie stopped rowing and lifted the oars from the water. They dripped into the river as he held them aloft, his eyes on her while she sprawled out on the thick wool blanket he kept in the back of his pickup truck.

They hadn't spent much time at the cabin, just long enough to put their bags inside and retrieve a complimentary picnic from the management that Robbie supplemented with a bottle of wine from Cambria Estates, a brand she hadn't heard of but which came from his relatives' vineyard in Australia.

"Of course." She settled her plastic wine cup into a holder notched into the wood near her seat.

He could ask her questions all day as long as she could just sit and watch him.

"You asked me once, 'Why me?' Do you

remember?" His dark hair gleamed in the sun like the coat of one of his horses.

She nodded. "I'd been feeling insecure about what a twenty-eight-year-old man could possibly see in a forty-year-old woman."

He grinned. "You know what they say about older women being at their sexual peak."

"Um. Yes. Well, as much as I appreciate that, I think you gave a more compelling answer the first time I asked that question in my condo." Her heart warmed at the memory of his sensitivity when he'd reeled off all kinds of things big and small that he liked about her. His answer had been insightful about what made her special. Unique.

They drifted down the river, back in the direction of the cabin. A small part of her didn't want the ride to end since everything about the boat trip had been perfect. They were quiet. Alone except for a handful of fishermen they'd passed.

Still, arriving back at the cabin meant she'd finally be able to touch him the way she'd longed to all day. The thought of all that raw male strength around her— inside her—made her knees weaker than the wine did.

"I'd like to turn that question around. You're a beautiful woman with great kids and the kind of quiet self-assurance that tells me you don't need a man in your life to be happy. What could you possibly find appealing in a horse trainer who—despite the family money—lives in a cabin with the carpets rolled up and shoots baskets in his free time?"

She watched him adjust the direction they were drifting with a deft move of the right oar.

"Is that how you see yourself?" She shook her head, disbelieving.

"I've got a temper, too. I'm not proud of it, but I lose my cool sometimes."

"Who doesn't?"

The oars dipped back into the water as they rounded a limestone ridge and their cabin came into sight.

He shrugged and Amanda realized he was serious. He genuinely viewed himself as a guy with too quick a temper and too much energy.

And wasn't it amazing how much a family could skew a person's self-image? Robbie didn't even appear to be aware of all he had to offer.

Amanda didn't know what the future held for her and Robbie, but she recognized the chance to give him something lasting, something that might stick with him long after he'd moved on to other stables, other horses and—much as it hurt—other women.

She turned backward in her seat as they drifted closer to the shore so she could help him pull the boat up onto the sand near their cabin. Once she jumped out and tugged the rowboat ashore with him, she gripped his hands in hers. Hiking boots sinking into the rocky mud, she stared up at him in the sunlight quickly turning to the dusky pinks and purples of twilight.

"I think you're an amazing man, Robbie Preston. And I can tell you exactly why." She squeezed his hands, her fingers sinking into his palms. "You see things below the surface in people and understand them the same way you seem to understand horses. I know you've taught me about my own son—aspects of his personality I didn't really see in the nine years I've been blessed to be his mother."

Robbie smiled, but he shook his head as if to refute the words. Amanda didn't give him a chance.

"And I can't quite explain how you did it, but you read my desires faster than any other man ever has, and I don't think that's just because I've wanted you more than I've ever wanted any man." She'd finally admitted that to herself, so there didn't seem to be any harm in sharing it with him. "I think it's because you look beyond people's words to read their body language and really perceive what makes them special. And I'll tell you what, if you hadn't pressed me into seeing you—knowing that I had feelings for you—I might still be sitting in my condo mourning an old life I'd never be able to recapture."

His mouth opened but no words came out. She'd surprised him and she was glad of it. Maybe he needed a wake-up call in his life as badly as she'd needed one in hers.

"And one more thing," she continued, wanting to make sure she got this right. "Thank you for that."

Leaning closer, she arched up on her toes to kiss him, hoping she'd given him something to think about long after tonight. Because right now, she didn't want to think or talk anymore.

Chapter Fourteen

Amanda Emory made one hell of a delicious armful.

Robbie had been totally unprepared for her kiss and it took him a minute to respond to the onslaught to his senses. He'd been physically seduced more than once in his life, but Amanda was the only woman who'd ever seduced his mind and—heaven help him—his heart.

You see things below the surface.

Her words had wrapped around him as surely as her soft vanilla scent did now. He sensed himself falling for her—a dangerous proposition with a woman who'd drawn careful boundaries—and still he gathered her against him and took over the kiss she'd begun so gently.

Lifting her up higher on his body, he aligned their mouths and cupped his hands around the soft curve of her bottom. Her head tipped back and he deepened the kiss, taking all that she offered and lobbying for more. Hotter. Deeper.

He explored the shape of her mouth and nipped at her damp lips, the heat inside him bursting into full-fledged flame. She tasted like merlot, tangy and intoxicating to his senses. His tongue dueled with hers until he could only think about tasting more of her. Tasting her everywhere.

Hitching her up in his arms, he raised her thighs to wrap around his body. He walked up the cobblestone path toward the secluded cabin in the heart of the Palisades, pausing to feel for the step so he didn't trip. Her arms wound around his neck, the friction of her body against his enough to make him dizzy. Lightheaded. Or maybe that was just every red blood cell sinking south as the intimate heat of her feminine core pressed tightly against his erection.

"Hurry," she whispered, voice edging toward frantic as she wriggled meaningfully against him. "I need you."

He shoved his way through the door to the tiny log cabin nestled among the cliffs. They'd left the porch light on before their rowboat trip and he used the illumination to find a switch in the main living area. Light flooded the simple space from a chandelier made of antlers and he pushed the dimmer switch down to soften the glare.

The cabin smelled of pine, the varnished walls covered in knots and photographs of boats on the river. He barely made it to the bedroom. His fingers couldn't get enough of her and he ran them up her back, tunneling under her T-shirt and lightweight jacket to span her skin. He unfastened her bra and sank down to sit on the patchwork quilt covering the massive rustic bed carved of split rails. She sprawled across his lap, her jeans taut against her thighs.

He had to have her out of them.

Robbie reached between them to unfasten the button and lower the zipper, exposing creamy soft skin. She sighed his name as she broke off the kiss, her head rolling back to expose her neck, the peace-sign pendant winking back at him.

He dipped his mouth to the flesh just below her jaw, drawing on it gently before he traced the chain of her necklace, the pendant clicking against his teeth. He wanted her to feel as desperate for him as he did for her, and the bedroom was his last resort. He'd bared more of his heart to her than anyone, and this intimacy was the only other way he could think of to reach her, to make her hunger for him on a soul-deep level.

Too bad she was already unfastening his belt buckle, unzipping his jeans and peeling away the denim barrier from his arousal. Her soft hands glanced over him, stroking away the layer of his boxers to trail a teasing touch over the head of him. The need to have her shuddered through him.

Oh, yeah, she was definitely an armful.

Knowing he'd be well on his way to mind-numbing bliss if her hands were any freer with his body, he lifted her up in his arms again and stood. Spinning around, he fell down onto the thick mattress, a bracing hand behind her back to take his weight off her as they sank into a pile of multi-colored pillows.

Her dark eyes widened, the smoldering look of sexual invitation burning him up from the inside out.

"What's the matter?" she whispered, her eyelids shuttering to half-mast as she rolled her hips beneath him. "Can't handle a woman in charge?"

Heat rushed through his veins, her teasing words no doubt serving their purpose as he thrust his hips into the hot juncture of her denim-covered thighs.

"Not when the woman is as red-hot as you." He'd let her be in charge later, when his teeth weren't on edge and his jaw wasn't sore from grinding them down to hold himself back. "So you're going to have to let me take the reins first."

She splayed a hand on his chest right above his racing heart. Her fingernails dug lightly into the fabric of his T-shirt.

"I've heard you young studs are all about speed and not always capable of full control." She lifted her head to nip his lower lip. "Is that true?"

He closed his eyes to shut out the vision of her mouth, softly swollen from his kisses. "If you're trying to fire me up, lady, you're doing one hell of a job."

"I want the same thing you do." She pulled his T-shirt up his back and wrestled it over his shoulders.

"Maybe." He caught her roving hands and pinned them to the bed long enough to regain control over his own need. "Except that I want to give you a pleasure you'll never forget first."

Her soft whimper told him she wasn't all that opposed to the idea. Drawing her hands up over her head, he held them there with one of his while he undressed her with the other.

Skimming her T-shirt up along with the bra he'd already unfastened, he took his time taking in the sight of her bare breasts, the peace-sign pendant now decorating the valley between them. Breathing lightly over one and then the other, he watched the nipples crest even tighter, the color darkening to the deepest pink. He took one in his mouth and suckled her, while her whole body undulated beneath him.

Never breaking that kiss, he reached down to push her jeans off her hips along with a pair of silky panties. Finally, only when he had her naked, did he release her hands.

"The good thing about a young stud is the tremendous amount of energy." He kissed a path down her belly to her hip while his hand stroked down her thighs, spreading them. "We can go all night without getting tired."

Her hips lifted off the bed when he placed a kiss between her legs. He breathed in the scent of her arousal, the sweetness threatening his control as much as her hands had earlier.

Delving deeper between her legs, he tasted her dampness, savored the delicate flesh as her thighs began to tremble against his restraining hands. She made incoherent sounds of pleasure while her fingers combed through his hair, her wordless cries urging him to search for that tender nub that could drive her over the edge.

When he drew upon the taut flesh she called his name with a hoarse shout, her body twisting underneath him until he had to hold her hips steady. Only then did she relax enough to let the feeling carry her away, her breath sinking into a harsh, fast rhythm until she unraveled. He could feel the soft ripples of her feminine flesh against his lips while she clenched her thighs tight.

When the trembling ceased he let her go and stretched out over her on the bed. He kissed her mouth, taking in her ragged breaths while he eased out of his jeans and boxers. He'd left his condoms in a prominent place on the nightstand since they'd both known what waited for them back at the cabin. He reached for one blindly now, feeling around until he found and unwrapped it. Sheathed himself.

"I have to confess," she whispered, her breathing still harsh, "I can see the benefit of a lot of energy."

He aligned himself with her as he stared down into her eyes.

"What if it means I don't let you sleep much tonight?"

"I wouldn't miss a second of my time with you." Something in that soft declaration clutched at his heart and he tried to distract himself with the sex that felt so freaking good.

Pressing his hips forward he entered her in one smooth stroke. He remained there, holding himself perfectly still while sweet little aftershocks from her orgasm pulsed against him. He hoped like hell he could make her feel this way again and again tonight, but for right now, he'd held back as long as he could.

The sense of possessiveness churning through him now was unlike anything he'd ever felt before. Wild and fierce, it brought an undeniable urgency into the room, a primal passion too strong to be contained.

Cradling her face with one hand, he kissed her. Hips pumping with a new, relentless rhythm, he gave himself over to desire until Amanda cried out all over again, her muscles tightening around him in a flurry of mind-blowing movements. He held himself steady for as long as he could, but it was like holding back the wind. His hips picked up the pace, aided by her slick heat. His release rushed him like a freight train, the force of it wracking his body until he was so spent he swore he saw stars.

Slumping to one side of her, he rolled Amanda toward him so he could see her in the light spilling in from the living room. In that brief, unguarded moment she looked as shell-shocked as he was, surprised by the impact of sex with so many building emotions threaded through it.

Or was he projecting his thoughts on her and seeing what he wanted to see?

Closing her eyes, she snuggled against him, pulling him close and shutting him out at the same time. And for that, Robbie couldn't deny an answering mix of disappointment and relief.

He was so lost in a tangle of conflicted feelings he almost missed the words she murmured into the sweat-slick flesh of his shoulder.

"A woman could get used to having a young stud around."

Happiness had always seemed like a fragile thing to Amanda, so right now she didn't want to do anything that might make the feeling disappear.

She didn't move. Didn't blink. Practically didn't breathe. She simply absorbed the sensation of Robbie's hard chest and hot skin beneath her cheek while she listened to his heart rate slow to a comforting pace.

She knew so much about this man. She hadn't taken time to get to know Dan before they married, a fact that had worked out because she'd been willing to compromise later in her marriage and she had loved him. But he'd dazzled her into marriage, making her laugh and appealing to her wild side until she wound up in a tiny house outside of L.A. with two kids, no degree and no one to blame but herself for her headlong approach to life.

With Robbie, she'd taken her time. Discovered multiple facets of him while she watched him in the context of his family. Her family. His work environment.

"I'm so glad your job isn't dangerous." She'd worried so much about Dan getting shot, worries that had proven well-founded even though she'd hated being right with all her heart.

"It must be hard being married to a cop." Robbie wrapped an arm around her and rubbed her back, his long fingers tracing slow, elaborate patterns on her bare skin.

"It wasn't bad when he was on street patrol, since the people he was busting were people like my roommate—mostly good kids who made a few bad decisions like trying recreational drugs or lifting purses at the bus station. Things got worse when he got promoted to a gang violence task force." She'd begged him not to take that job, her sixth sense breaking out into hives.

She'd sworn she would have been more understanding about that kind of career move if Dan had waited until Max was at least ten years old, but her husband had been passionately committed to his job. As much as she told herself he was a good cop and she should have supported him in a responsibility he took so seriously, she found it hard to forgive him when his choice meant the boys had so few years with their father.

She burrowed deeper into Robbie's chest, needing the comfort of his heartbeat close to hers.

"How did things get out of hand the night he died? Didn't he have back-up?"

A chill chased down her spine at the memory.

"He'd gotten a tip there would be a drug deal, but his informant failed to appreciate the scope of the exchange." Or so the police report had said. She'd regretted reading it, but she'd insisted, certain Kevin had left out some part of Dan's final hours. "There were dealers from overseas and they weren't just selling drugs, they were trading the drugs for weapons, so my husband walked into a miniature arsenal and extra manpower."

Robbie dropped a kiss on the top of her head and she closed her eyes, concentrating on that warm contact.

"Dan took out two of the foreigners who went for the guns, but he didn't see Brad Orway and his brother Benny coming toward him. Brad shot Dan while Benny fired at Kevin. Dan managed to hit Brad, who also died at the scene. Benny watched his brother bleed out while Kevin put the cuffs on him." She'd made Kevin tell her the logistics over and over again even though she'd known it wasn't fair to force him to relive the night. But at least he'd seen what happened. He'd been able to say goodbye to Dan.

"I can't believe the brother is out of jail already."

"Especially when he threatened me at the trial, but you know how that goes—they can't do anything until the bastard actually comes after me."

Robbie positioned himself so he could look in her eyes.

"Do you have a restraining order?"

"Yes. Dan's whole precinct was very good about

seeing I had as much protection as they could give me, but bottom line, until he actually tries to hurt me, they can't help any more."

"I wish—" He broke off, shaking his head. His whole body had tensed and she wasn't sure when that happened. His eyes, however, were filled with a compassion that warmed her.

"What?"

"I wish I wasn't going to Texas next week. I set up an interview for a head trainer position on Monday and I planned to leave Sunday night."

"You're breaking away from Quest?" Perhaps she shouldn't be shocked. And it really wasn't her business since she'd been the one drawing boundaries all around her new life and her fragile heart.

Still, she couldn't help feeling just a little bit… betrayed, somehow. She should have held tighter to the happiness she'd experienced earlier in the day since she of all people knew that emotion was fragile. The bitter reality of this reminder stung.

"I can't stay in an environment where my judgment is questioned and my talents are unappreciated. I know I'm worth more than my father is willing to see, so I'd never be able to really thrive here anyhow."

"Maybe he just needs some more time. Or maybe when Something to Talk About wins that Sandstone Derby in Dubai next month—"

"But I don't want to tie my success to the success of a long-shot horse. I believe in Something to Talk About, but why should the colt's win sway my dad's opinion?" He shrugged, the gesture a sad statement of resignation for a relationship he couldn't fix. "I've trained a steady stream of respected racers and my stats for winners are better than any other trainer in the stables. But no winning percentage will make up for the fact that my dad still sees a stubborn kid when he looks at me."

"You belong here." She said it to herself as much as him, the words more an observation than an argument.

Still, she could feel the resistance in him and hear it in his words.

"I belong wherever I can be effective in my job."

"No, I— That is, I agree." She just couldn't begin to imagine her life without this strong and passionate man in it. "You're too good at what you do to waste your talents. I just think it's a shame since you seem so much a part of Quest."

"Yeah?" He wrapped his arms around her, his big, gorgeous body already coming alive again. "I gotta say you're the only one who sees it that way, Ms. Emory. Most of the rest of the folks around the stables see me as the black sheep who refuses to go away—at least so far."

She shook her head, her skin tingling with the promise of more pleasure at his hands.

"You've been locked in this conflict with your dad for so long maybe you don't see the way the rest of the staff looks at you. But trust me, people listen when you speak. Kiefer had you pegged for the man in charge after his first day at the stables and you know how kids see things the rest of us don't."

She debated trying to talk him into staying. Heck, she'd been so concerned how her boys would feel if she got involved with a man who backed out of their relationship. Now she wondered if she should have been preparing for how *she'd* feel. Because she had a feeling the hole Robbie Preston would leave in her heart wouldn't be filled any time soon.

"I don't know if you're right about anyone sitting up to pay attention when I talk, but I'd just be content tonight if *you'd* listen when I speak." He nipped her shoulder with his teeth.

If this was to be one of her few nights with him, she wouldn't squander it by missing him already. She'd thrown herself too deep in the world of the living to bury herself in sadness when a vibrant, seductive man shared her bed for at least a few more hours.

"Depends what kinds of things you have to say to me."

"Oh, I don't know. Maybe I'd tell you when I want you to kiss me." He grazed his lips across her mouth with slow deliberation.

She started to think she could set her worries aside for this.

"Or touch me." He guided her hand to his arousal and she wrapped her fingers around the silken heat of him.

"You've made your point." Tracing the thick vein up his shaft with her fingertip, she wished they could play like this for weeks or months instead of hours. "And yes, you can count me among those who pay attention when you speak. Although you'd better hope no one else is hearing quite the same words as me."

She didn't know where the surge of possessiveness came from, but she meant every word.

"Never," he promised, and she wished with all her heart that could be true.

Chapter Fifteen

Robbie sped east through rolling green hills past one horse farm after another. The ride back to Quest was a lot more subdued than their trip out to Keeneland had been the day before.

Despite the fact they'd made love all night long, and she'd admitted she'd never felt so good in all her life, Amanda hadn't given any indication that she wanted to change the parameters of their take-it-slow arrangement, an arrangement that probably excluded her packing up and moving to Texas with him.

They'd left in a hurry this morning after Amanda had received a call from a cop in L.A. who'd heard a rumor that Benny Orway might have skipped town. Amanda had called Claudia right away to check on her boys and they were fine, but Robbie didn't blame her for wanting to get home. He was eager to check on the kids, too, a fact that reminded him how much he already cared about her whole family.

He glanced sideways at her in the passenger seat of his brother's truck, short dark hair blowing around her cheeks and teasing her jawline. She stared out the window, lost in thoughts where he couldn't join her, and he hated that their whole relationship had been put on hold because of his stalling career. If he weren't looking for a position outside of Quest, it would be easier to see her quietly on the weekends, keeping their relationship away from the boys until they had a better idea of whether they had what it took for something more long-term. That would make Amanda happy because she wouldn't be risking her boys getting attached to a man who would leave, and it would make him happy to be with her.

Well, he'd be happy in his personal life but suffocating in the job he'd trained for since he was a child.

"You could come to Texas with me."

He didn't know how he'd let the thought slip, but it brought Amanda's head whipping around in his direction.

"Excuse me?" She straightened in her seat, a bewildered half smile on her face.

He hadn't meant even to speak the words aloud, his half-formed idea only just coming together as he steered the heavy-duty pickup off the exit for Quest Stables. But he'd spoken it just the same, and now

Amanda stared at him as though he'd just suggested she take a trip with him to Outer Mongolia.

"I was just thinking about you and the boys here at Quest while I'm alone in Texas." He was already hurting this morning at the idea of leaving her and he hadn't even dropped her off at her cabin yet. What would it be like when he couldn't reach over and touch her the way he did right now?

He gave her forearm a squeeze, reminding himself she still occupied the seat beside him and that he could still touch her if he needed to.

"You deserve this, Robbie." She gazed at him with that all-wise look of hers that made him wonder how he'd gotten lucky enough to know her, to hold her hostage in his bed for hours on end. "Go to Texas and knock their socks off."

"But what I was trying to say was—" He glanced over at her and hesitated. "You could always come to Texas with me if I took the job. I know that sounds crazy based on the amount of time we've known each other, but you're no stranger to making unexpected choices and taking the road less traveled, right?"

He sensed rather than saw her shaking her head on the other side of the cab, but he was in too deep now to turn back. He'd taken the plunge, so he might as well keep going even if he was in *way* over his head.

"We've got something special, Amanda, and the whole pile of our differences doesn't add up to half the magnitude of everything that's right about us." His math might be wobbly there, but he was on a roll.

"Best of all, if you go to Texas you can put one more move between you and the creep who threatened you. You'd be all the harder to find."

He would keep her and the boys safe no matter what.

"It's tempting to run," she admitted, her voice low and serious. "But I could spend my whole life running and not be safe."

"You'd be safer." He turned down the road to Quest Stables, the long stretch of pavement feeling way too short when the dissolution of his relationship with Amanda waited at the other end.

"But would you really want that to be the reason I moved halfway across the country with you? To be safe from a vengeful lunatic?" She clasped her hands tight in her lap and he could feel the tension in the truck.

His. Hers.

And damn it all, but he had no idea where it was coming from even though it had snowballed into this massive cloud of negative energy.

"I want you to be safe," he insisted, knowing he had a point.

Did she really expect him to make a declaration of undying affection when she'd only view that kind of thing with skepticism? Or was he missing the bigger picture and not seeing what she wanted at all?

"I do, too, but I'm not willing to sacrifice my happiness for safety and, well, I couldn't be happy living like that."

She drew blood with that one.

"You couldn't be happy with me?" He slowed

down as they passed the office building and the corrals to drive toward the staff cabins so Amanda could pick up the boys at Claudia's.

"I can't accept a wild-ride relationship anymore, Robbie. I went through the roller-coaster romance with my husband and—" She took a deep breath. "I want something that goes deeper this time."

He didn't have a clue what to say in response to that. "I'm sorry—"

"No." He didn't want her pity. "Don't even think about being sorry. I had a great time with you and I'd prefer to think you enjoyed yourself too."

He pulled up at Claudia's cabin and cut the engine. "I did."

"Good. I just wish you of all people could have seen that maybe I do have something deeper to offer." He wasn't just a wild ride. "You seem so quick to defend my readiness to take on a head trainer job, but you refuse to see that I might have something more substantial to offer you. Something deeper, as you say."

He hit the steering wheel with the heel of his hand as Max came running out of Claudia's house to see his mother. Their time alone together was officially over, and all bets were off for how much he'd be able to see her in the future.

The troubled expression on her face tweaked his conscience, but damn it, he hurt too. He admired the way she stuffed her feelings away as she pried open the truck's passenger door and scavenged up a smile for her younger son.

"Maxie!" she called, holding her arms out to the dark-haired boy with flour handprints on his shirt, likely from a baking project.

God, she was an amazing mom. She'd brought the kids two thousand miles from the rest of her family to buy them peace and safety, and still the boys seemed happy. Well-adjusted. He knew that didn't happen by accident two years after they'd lost their father. She must have worked hard to give them that solid sense of family.

"Where's Kiefer?" Amanda asked, peering around the fenced yard of Claudia's cabin, where a handful of other kids were playing outside on the tire swing.

"Don't be mad at him, Mom." Max stepped out of the hug, his expression shifting from elated to worried.

Instantly alert, Robbie opened the driver's door and came around the pickup.

Amanda touched Max's face, a gentle stroke even though Robbie could see the worry in her eyes.

"I won't be mad, baby. Is Kiefer watching movies with bad words?" Her gaze darted around the yard again and Robbie didn't waste any time going to Claudia's door to call for Kiefer.

Amanda was right behind him, tugging Max along with her.

"He's not watching movies, Mom. But he made me promise not to tell." Max's whisper was loud enough for Robbie to hear and he hoped that meant the boy was eager to clue them in.

Claudia came into the small foyer of the cabin, wiping her hands on her flour-covered apron. The whole house smelled like sugar cookies.

"What's the matter?" Claudia asked. Her son—the Marine—sat at the kitchen table painting round cookies with orange and yellow paint to look like pumpkins.

All eyes went to Max while the Marine rose from his seat and jogged into a back room. Checking for Kiefer?

"Kiefer is watching videos," Claudia replied. "He took a movie into the bedroom when Max and I started to make cookies—" She hurried toward the bedroom as well, perhaps wondering why the boy hadn't come out to greet his mother.

Robbie's heart slammed in his chest and he reached to steady Amanda as she squeezed Max's hand and spoke to him softly.

"It's very important to tell Mommy where Kiefer went. We need to watch out for each other all the time, remember?"

Max's eyes welled with tears and Robbie could hear the Marine calling for Kiefer in the back of the house, the guy's voice getting louder with each holler.

"Mommy, he really wanted to go on the horse-back-riding trip. He said he was just going to the stable to wave goodbye to the other kids."

The Marine emerged from the back rooms, the guy's tortured expression saying it all.

"I'm sorry, Amanda." He shook his head. "I can't find Kiefer, and the bedroom window is open. I'd locked it from the inside, but he must have unlatched it and hopped out into the flower bed."

Robbie felt the kick to his solar plexus and Kiefer wasn't even his kid. He couldn't imagine how worried Amanda must be. Wrapping an arm around her, he gestured toward Claudia's phone.

"Call Fred's cell phone and check whether he's seen him." He scribbled his own cell phone number on a scrap of paper from his pocket and handed it to the Marine. "Call us if Kief comes back here, and we'll head over to Fred's place." He kissed the top of Amanda's head and steered her toward the door. "We're going to find him."

Amanda wouldn't have made it to the truck if Robbie hadn't steered her there.

Her whole body had gone numb when Max said Kiefer had left. Sneaked out of the house while his babysitter thought he was watching a movie.

She'd rushed out of Claudia's house to find him, but she hadn't even known where to go. She wasn't familiar with the old barn that Fred would use as a meeting place for the kids going on the horseback-riding trip. Quest Stables housed hundreds of horses in buildings all over the grounds.

"This way." Robbie pointed her toward his pickup and opened the door. He gave her a gentle nudge up to the running board. "It's quicker to drive there."

Apparently her brain had gone numb too, because she couldn't think. Couldn't dare to let herself feel the weight of worry about her son. Her first-born. One of the precious lives she'd been charged with protecting when Dan died. He'd probably just run off to see Fred and the others on the horseback-riding trip since she hadn't let him attend the event. But it was a mother's instinct to worry, to paint worst-case scenarios. Her lower lip trembled and she bit it hard to stop the shaking. If she lost control now, she'd never get out from under the debilitating panic.

"I shouldn't have left." She watched out the window for any signs of her son's familiar green eyes and sun-tipped hair. "I should have been here to make sure they were safe."

Robbie's hand reached across the pickup's cab to squeeze hers in a powerful grip.

"He could have just as easily slipped out on your watch. It's not like someone knocked on the door and physically took him, and that's what we were worried about. That's what you safeguarded him against by having him stay with Claudia while her son was home."

"I won't be able to stand it if anything happens to him." Her pocket started ringing and she realized it was her cell phone. A quick scan of the caller ID told her it was Claudia's house. She pressed the on button. "Did you find him?"

She switched the phone to Speaker so Robbie could hear as they drove up a small hill past some workmen repainting the split rail fence.

"No, but I wanted to tell you there's no answer on Fred's cell phone and that's highly unusual."

Pain twisted through the numbness inside her.

"We're almost at Fred's place now," Robbie interjected, releasing Amanda's hand as he made a hard turn.

"Do you want me to call your parents and ask them to spread the word?" Claudia asked. "If all of us look for him—"

"Yes. My mom and dad will mobilize every person on the property within the next thirty minutes when they hear he's missing. Thanks, Claudia."

"Is this it?" Amanda disconnected the call as Robbie stopped the truck in front of a low stable building that looked to be older than the bigger facilities near the offices. The white paint job matched the rest of the property, however, marking the place as part of the Prestons' sprawling domain.

"Yes. And I know you want to race in there, but let me go first." He looked her in the eye and she felt a warm rush of gratitude to him for being here with her. Still, his fears must mirror her own if he wanted to enter the building ahead of her.

Amanda didn't have any reason to think the gang that had shot Dan had taken up residence around Quest Stables, but obviously she wasn't the only one who could play the what-if game when it came to the kids. Robbie was thinking the same thing. What if Kiefer had chosen the wrong day to take off on his own?

"Yes. I'll be right behind you." She kissed him hard on the cheek. "Be careful."

He nodded. "We'll find him."

She clung to those words, replaying them over and over in her head as she followed Robbie out of the pickup and across the lawn toward the stable building. The place seemed unnaturally quiet and the main doors were closed. No horses stood in the stalls that faced them, although there might be animals on the other side in the fenced area beyond the structure. Or, for all she knew, maybe this particular building was just used for a meeting place now that Quest had more upscale facilities closer to the main exercise yard.

She held her breath as Robbie opened the door and stood to one side of the jamb. He wrapped an arm across her mid-section, pinning her in place against the wall while he peeked inside.

"Oh, shit." He sped into motion, releasing her and racing inside the building.

Amanda's heart sank as she hurried behind him. Kids lay on the floor of the stable with their hands covering their heads, as if someone had told them to lie still and not make any noise. There were twitches and soft sobs, however, that told her none of them had been hurt.

She knew with a glance that her son was not among these children.

"Amanda, Fred looks like he took a hell of a blow to the head." Robbie cradled the older man's shoulders and she could see where the ranch hand's temple bled.

Fred lay apart from the kids, closer to the door, so she hadn't seen him initially. His limbs were at an awkward angle to his wiry frame.

"Boys and girls, you're going to be safe now, but you have to tell us what happened here." Amanda wanted to reassure the children, but she also wanted to find her son before anything happened to him. "Did anyone see Kiefer?"

Two little girls were clutching each other and crying in earnest, but the rest of the group appeared too shell-shocked to process whatever had happened here.

An older boy, a young teen as tall as Amanda, rose to his feet. He wore a Quest Stables T-shirt and she guessed he was probably supposed to be helping Fred supervise the horseback-riding trip.

"Ma'am, your son came around the stables to see the horses about a half hour ago." He shoved his blue ball cap back on his head, his fingers scratching at the dark hair beneath. "He was here for just a few minutes when a man ran into the stable with a gun, demanding to know which kid was Kiefer."

A lump grew in Amanda's throat but she forced it down in order to keep her focus. She needed her wits about her if she was going to find her son. Images of her little boy's face flashed through her mind—a montage of moments from birth to yester-day—plaguing her with a mother's instinct to save him at any cost.

"We wouldn't have told him," a ponytailed girl called out from the other side of the room. She was tall and slim but probably not much older than Kiefer. Her fists were clenched tight as she spoke. "But Kiefer stood right up when he threatened the two littlest ones."

She pointed to the two girls still crying in the middle of the room and Amanda got her feet in motion to give them each a comforting hug. For that matter, maybe she was seeking some comfort herself. She felt so brittle inside she feared she would shatter any moment.

"It's okay," she murmured to the girls while Robbie phoned the local police.

After giving them the information, he tucked the phone away.

"Did the man have a vehicle?" He was on his feet and by her side, his hand gripping one shoulder for a squeeze as he quizzed the older boy in the ball cap.

"No. He left on foot heading north. Fred tried to stop him but the guy hit him with the butt of his gun and told us all we'd better not make a sound or he'd come back and kill us. I was going to wait two more minutes and then use the phone in Fred's office."

Robbie was already heading for the door, boots pounding the floor so hard she could swear she felt his resolution through to her soul. God, as much as she wanted to be independent, she needed his strength now.

"He can't have gone far. Stay with Fred and call the EMTs. I'm going after them."

Amanda's heart surged painfully, hope and dread warring. Having been married to a police officer, she knew the official stance should have been for civilians to let the cops handle the matter. But a cold-blooded gangster bent on revenge had her son. She couldn't find it in her heart to ask Robbie to wait.

She ran out of the stable after him, if only to watch him leave. He had his head inside a beat-up old pickup truck covered in dust. Squinting into the setting sun, she could see he reached for something across the back windshield.

He emerged holding a shotgun and a wave of hope fortified her. Robbie wasn't walking into this fight blind the way her husband had the night of his death when he'd expected a drug deal and discovered a weapons trade along with it. Robbie would match firepower with Orway if necessary.

"Be safe!" She called to him as he hustled across the yard toward a corral full of saddled horses the kids must have been planning to ride. "This man is dangerous."

Robbie looked over the horses carefully and seemed to know which one to choose before he mounted up. He handled the long firearm so easily she guessed he was no stranger to that kind of weapon.

And at that most inconceivable of moments, she knew she loved him. The reputed quick-tempered ways of his youth had matured into a steely resolve and the ability to act quickly and decisively. This was a man you could count on. A man to respect. A man to love.

"Orway might be deadly on the streets of L.A., but the Kentucky hills are my backyard." He'd backed the horse up in the crowded pen, and somehow the other animals knew to move to one side to clear him a path.

He kicked the horse's side and it bolted, running

so fast toward the split-rail fence Amanda tensed. At the last second, the bay mare went airborne, leaping over the barrier easily before hitting the ground on the other side and galloping into the trees on the northern side of the stables.

Winging a prayer heavenward for Robbie and her son's safe return, Amanda hurried back into the stable.

Sirens sounded in the distance.

Robbie hoped it wouldn't make his quarry all the more antsy since it had to be difficult for the guy to navigate his way through the woods with a kid in tow. Robbie had left his horse once he found the path Orway had taken and was certain he was close. He didn't want the sound of approaching hooves to give the gangster any advantage.

He couldn't fail in this.

Part of him felt certain he could overpower the kidnapper easily. But the other part of him kept hearing his father's voice tell him how foolish he was to continuously take big risks. Was this one of those times when he should have waited before jumping in?

He didn't think so. Amanda's terrified expression when she'd heard Kiefer had been taken really made the decision for him. How could he let her suffer that way if there was a chance he could get Kiefer back? He hadn't ridden and hunted these hills all his life for nothing. He'd bet he could find the boy faster than anyone else with the help of a good horse, and here he was, creeping silently through a thicket while his quarry crashed through the weeds some ten yards ahead of him.

Ever since he'd mounted up back at the old stable, Robbie had worried about finding Kiefer hurt—or worse—along the gangster's escape route. So he was relieved now to feel the thump of two sets of footprints on the ground ahead of him.

Thank you, God.

The guy was headed the wrong way if he hoped to get back to the road, and that's probably what he'd meant to do. As it was, escape would be cut off by a ravine on one side and an old fence meant to keep in escaped horses on the other. So although an interstate ran by here, there would be no access from this direction unless Orway brought wire cutters.

The sirens sounded closer now, as if the police had driven through the winding roads of Quest to access the back stables where Fred and the kids had been found. Robbie might be able just to wait and watch over Kiefer to be sure Orway didn't hurt him.

No. Whether it was foolish to push his luck, Robbie wouldn't let Amanda's son suffer in fear one second longer than he had to. Her love for her sons was one of the most beautiful things he'd ever seen in life and he planned to protect that. Orway had vowed revenge on the family, so the guy could decide to wreak it any moment.

Robbie climbed a tall pine tree that he'd once built a deer stand in with his brothers. And sure enough, an old piece of plank board was still nailed between a few of the branches about fifteen feet up.

From this vantage point he could see Kiefer and Orway. The kid walked a few feet in front of Orway, a blindfold on his eyes as he stumbled down a small hill. Orway was a wiry man of medium build wearing a pair of nylon track pants that were getting caught on every bush he walked past. He held a gun in one hand and what looked like a cell phone in the other.

Red-faced and panting, the man appeared frustrated. Angry. Lost in the woods and plenty pissed about it. Robbie lowered his eye to his scope to keep an eye on the guy.

Just as Benny Orway lifted his weapon.

Chapter Sixteen

Robbie didn't have time to weigh pros and cons. He couldn't guess Orway's intent. But there was a handgun trained on Amanda's son while the kid wandered ten feet ahead—blindfolded and unaware of the threat.

Thanking God for the distance between the bastard and the boy, Robbie flipped off the safety just as Orway must have heard some rustle in the trees above them. He turned, spinning just sideways of the scope on the shotgun as his eyes found Robbie in the tree stand.

This shot wouldn't kill the guy. But, oh, man, it was going to hurt like a son of a bitch. Lowering his weapon by a fraction of an inch to find his target, Robbie made the shot that would free Kiefer.

* * *

Gunfire split the air.

Amanda would have passed out cold if Jenna Preston hadn't been by her side, holding her hand tightly as they stood next to one of three police cars that had arrived on the scene about five minutes prior.

Robbie's family had driven out to the old stable from every corner of the property. Claudia hadn't been kidding about mobilizing everyone in residence at Quest. Apparently Robbie's two older brothers had elected to sit outside Claudia's house to make sure Orway didn't try to come back for Max, while Robbie's parents had come out to the stable to comfort the kids and frantic parents who'd heard what had happened.

"You said Robbie took Fred's shotgun, right?" Thomas Preston was a hard and uncompromising man by all accounts, but Amanda had seen only a kind man who had Robbie's blue eyes.

He'd been at the stable before the EMTs arrived and had spoken reassuring words to the older ranch hand as Fred started coming around.

"Yes." Amanda squeezed her eyes shut for another prayer, her millionth in the last twenty minutes. "I saw him take it out of Fred's truck."

Thomas nodded, his craggy face tipped toward the northern woods where police were already searching for Kiefer on foot. Only two of the six officers who'd answered the call felt comfortable tackling the job on horseback, but the Prestons had offered mounts to anyone who wanted one. And while Amanda suspected these weren't million-dollar Thoroughbreds to start with, she appreciated the offer of well-trained animals to aid in the hunt.

"Well, that was a shotgun firing, no question."

Amanda shook off the offer of coffee from a woman who'd set up an industrial-sized pot inside the stable building. And she never would have believed she could have taken any comfort from anything or anyone while Orway held Kiefer and threatened to shatter her world all over again. But having friends around her now—other mothers who appeared every bit as scared for her son as she was—bolstered her.

She peered up at Thomas, but he was already engaged in conversation with an officer who'd stayed behind to coordinate the search efforts and ask questions.

Amanda waited for the police radio to squawk with some sort of news, an officer's report that a shot was fired—anything. But then, glancing back to the treeline at the base of the hill, she saw him.

Them.

"Kiefer!" Her heart nearly burst at the sight of Robbie's horse racing out of the woods.

The big bay carried Robbie with Kiefer perched in front of him on the saddle. Whole. Smiling, if a little pale.

She let go of Jenna's hand to plow through the other parents milling around, past the police cars and the horse corral to fly down the hill like a woman possessed. The horse covered far more distance than she did and she met them in no time. Kiefer slid out of the saddle and she half caught him, stumbling with his weight.

"My baby." She hugged him tight, tears spilling down her cheeks in full-fledged rivers, all the emotion she'd held back pouring out to soak his denim jacket.

"I'm okay. Honest, Mom. I'm okay." Kiefer patted her head with awkward tenderness. "I'm sorry I left Ms. Claudia's house."

Behind Kiefer she heard Robbie telling the officer on site about Orway's location, but at the same time the officer's handheld radio crackled to life with a report that they'd found the suspect and needed an ambulance for a bullet wound to the man's left foot.

Amanda rose to stand, still clutching Kiefer in a half-hug while she strode toward Robbie. The crowd of other parents had followed the action down the hill despite the commanding officer's plea to keep the scene clear.

"Robbie." Amanda reached for him with her free arm, needing to assure herself he was alive and well. Unharmed.

She knew what it felt like to lose a loved one to violence and she would never take any of the incredible males in her life for granted.

"We got him back." Robbie managed a half smile for her benefit, but she could see the shadows that still lurked in his eyes.

He'd been scared for Kiefer.

She didn't know how she understood that, but she did. This strong, smart, kind-hearted man had been every bit as worried about her son as she had.

"No, Robert Preston." She threw herself into his arms, releasing Kiefer to hold Robbie and thank him properly. "*You* got him back. You saved his life and I will never forget the debt I owe you, even if it's too huge for me ever to repay."

Robbie squeezed her harder, burying his face in her hair while one of the EMTs on site spoke quietly to Kiefer behind her.

"I couldn't let anything happen to your son. I told you I'd keep you and the boys safe, and I meant that whether you want to come to Texas with me or not."

She wanted to tell him that she loved him and would follow him to the ends of the earth, but people were crowding around them. Amanda heard Jenna making soft little sobbing sounds—good sobbing—and it occurred to her another mother had been terrified for her son today.

Amanda released Robbie to see both Jenna and Thomas standing close by. Jenna flung herself into Robbie's arms, squeezing him tight, while Thomas folded up his cell phone.

"I just talked to Brent and Andrew," he told Amanda. "They're going to bring Max over so he can see his brother, if that's okay with you."

For her answer, Amanda hugged him too.

"You and Jenna have been so good to me. Thank you

so much." When she stood back, the older man's cheeks flushed brighter than they'd been a moment ago.

"Jenna's always said we're like family at Quest." He stared over at his wife holding on to the son he'd never seen eye-to-eye with. "That's more because of her than me, but it's not because I don't think so, too."

Amanda understood him better than he thought.

"Mrs. Emory?" The EMT who'd been speaking to Kiefer turned toward her. "I'd like to take Kiefer up to the ambulance to retrieve a few things for him so we can get him in the stable before—" he leaned closer and lowered his voice "—the police bring up the stretcher with the shooting victim."

"Yes." Amanda nodded to Thomas and left the Prestons to walk up the hill with Kiefer. No way in hell did she want him to see Benny Orway again. "Thank you. Kiefer's not hurt, is he?"

She wondered if she hadn't looked him over carefully enough.

Around the stable, parents were leaving with their children, no doubt for the same reason—they didn't want their kids to see the man who'd threatened them all. The adults who worked at Quest and didn't have children involved in the horseback-riding trip remained on site, unsaddling the horses the kids had planned to ride and putting up the tack.

"He's fine, ma'am." The EMT—a tall young man in a navy-blue uniform—patted her son's shoulder. "But we're going to give him a puff off the oxygen tank to power him up and I'm going to try and talk him into a stuffed bear to commemorate the day he tangled with an outlaw."

Kiefer looked up at her, his green eyes sheepish.

"It's *not* a teddy bear." He had a dirt smudge across his forehead and a small scratch along his temple where he probably had come in contact with a tree branch, but other than that he looked good.

Strong. Healthy. And not terribly traumatized.

Thank you, Robbie Preston.

"I'm sure it's not, but it would be good to share with Max. He feels terrible he let you leave Ms. Claudia's." She would talk to him in more detail about what had happened—and his role in facilitating what Orway did—another time. Right now she just wanted to get him home and feel safe knowing the threat to them all would go from a hospital floor to a prison ward.

Kiefer's face clouded while the EMT disappeared into the back of the ambulance. At the bottom of the hill near the treeline she could see a stretcher emerging from the trees.

Orway.

Her blood went cold even if she couldn't see his face and he was laid out with a bullet wound.

"Mom, I was so scared that man would hurt all the other kids. And I led him right to them all."

Amanda watched the EMT hop down from the treatment area of the ambulance with a rolling oxygen tank in one hand and a blanket and two bears in the other.

Amanda followed him into the stable, as eager to hide from the sight of Orway as anyone.

"It wasn't your fault he threatened those children any more than it was your father's fault he came after you." Amanda hoped that logic made some sort of sense, but she thought maybe she'd better let Kiefer speak to a counselor after this was all over to be sure he didn't carry around a boatload of undeserved guilt. "Orway is a bad man and he's responsible for threatening your friends."

She guided him into the stable just as another car pulled up behind the police cruisers.

"But he hurt Mr. Fred." Tears welled in Kiefer's eyes.

"Mr. Fred is fine." Amanda held open the door, waiting to see if the arriving party included Max and Robbie's brothers. "He went to the hospital just to double-check, but he was awake and asking about you before he left. Believe me, he was every bit as scared for you as you were for him."

"Max!" Kiefer spotted his little brother before Amanda did and he shook off the blanket from his EMT buddy to run out and greet him.

He nearly slammed into one of Robbie's older brothers' legs before the guy—Brent, she thought—steered him around to one side. Max and Kiefer met in a hug that more resembled a body slam, but she could see the fierce brotherly love in their tight squeeze.

Behind her, she sensed Robbie's approach and she wondered when she'd started feeling his presence before she laid eyes on him. Turning, she moved toward him without even thinking, realizing she suddenly stood in the ring of his arms, surrounded by all of his family except for Melanie. Thomas and Jenna clasped hands a few steps behind Robbie.

Amanda could see the stretcher was being loaded into the ambulance, but the back of the emergency vehicle remained hidden from view with the help of two big doors and a throng of police officers.

"Did Mr. Robbie really shoot the guy who wanted to hurt you?"

Max's incredulous words suddenly rose over the din of conversation, police radios and the occasional neigh of an uneasy horse.

Amanda's gaze flew to Robbie's brothers and Brent shrugged.

"I hope that was okay, Ms. Emory. He was awfully worried about his brother, and I thought that would ease his mind." He offered his hand. "I'm Brent, by the way. I've heard a lot about your son from my daughters."

"Of course. Thank you." Belatedly, Amanda remembered hearing Brent had lost his wife. She greeted both Andrew—a tall, more serious-looking man who took after his father—and Brent, who was the picture of sun-bronzed athleticism. Kiefer regaled Max with the story of Robbie's heroism, concentrating on being rescued instead of on his capture, which must have been terrifying. She regretted that Kiefer had grown up quickly in so many ways these last two years, but she heartened at the sight of him clutching a stuffed bear beneath one arm. He wore the EMT's blanket like a super hero's cape.

Thomas cleared his throat and stepped forward.

"We're all headed up to the big house for dinner." He lowered his head like a man used to looking over the tops of his glasses as he spoke, even though he didn't wear any. "Ms. Emory, that means you and the boys, too. The police are going to search the grounds tonight to make sure Orway didn't have an accomplice, but they've already cleared the main house so you'll be safe there tonight."

Amanda's eyes went to Robbie since she didn't plan on going anywhere without him. She had so much to say to him. Would he attend a meal at his parents' house even though he'd shunned the idea of taking Amanda to the family cocktail hour in the past?

He gave a nod and she knew he would be there with her tonight. She was grateful except that they'd have an audience she was just barely getting to know. Would there be any time to get him alone and talk to him before he set off for his interview in Texas the next day?

As much as Amanda might enjoy the warmth of his family around them, she knew Robbie had never thrived in that environment. She would follow him wherever he chose to go if he would still have her, but she couldn't help but think they were already living in the best, safest home she could imagine.

Chapter Seventeen

Robbie wondered if he'd lost his touch with reading people since he couldn't guess what was going on in Amanda's mind beneath that reserved facade of hers.

She looked beautiful in a simple dress his mother had borrowed from Melanie's closet since Amanda's clothes were soiled and bloodstained from providing first aid to Fred before the EMTs arrived. The outfit his mother had chosen for her was in a soft knit fabric in deep blue with a long skirt and a wide neckline that left plenty of room for her peace-sign necklace. His California girl.

He knew he could never ask her to go to Texas with him if he got that job now. Not when she felt so obligated and grateful to him that she might relocate just because he'd saved Kiefer. He didn't think she would do that, but the next move she made needed to originate fully from her own wishes, not something he'd nudged her into.

"Melanie called," Thomas announced as they sat down at the long dining-room table where salads awaited them. Candles burned and extra containers of fresh flowers dotted the center of the table, marking the occasion as a special one. "She said if we can wait five minutes she'll be able to join us."

Robbie tensed in his seat next to Amanda, his focus on his father even as he leaned over to speak to Amanda. He lowered his voice while his mother moved around the table, pouring a glass of red wine for each adult as a server poured a second glass of white.

"Melanie was at the race with Something to Talk About today," Robbie reminded her.

Behind them, Kiefer and Max sat at a small table for the kids with Brent's daughters, Katie and Rhea. Robbie could hear the boys asking for more milk, and although Katie jumped up to retrieve the pitcher, the server who'd been pouring the wine beat her to it.

Amanda reached for his hand beneath the table and whispered back to him.

"Do you think your father knows the outcome of the race and isn't telling?" Her dark eyes darted from Robbie to his father and back.

God, he wished he had a normal family life for her sake. He would stay at Quest in a heartbeat if not for the strained relationship between him and his father and the lack of professional respect.

"Hard to tell with the old man." Stretching, Robbie reached around the back of Amanda's chair to align his arm just above her shoulders. Not exactly touching, but close.

He wanted to touch her. Badly. To claim her for his own in front of his brothers and parents and anyone else who took even a remote interest in his life. But he hadn't had two seconds alone with her since they'd finished answering questions from the police and come back to the main house to clean up.

"I'm sorry I'm late!" Melanie burst into the room in jeans and a sweatshirt, her face scrubbed clean and her hair wet. She looked like a college co-ed.

Robbie had never been able to read Melanie as easily as he could read other people, so he wasn't sure what the outcome of the day had been from her expression.

Now she hurried around to the far side of the table and hugged Amanda.

"I heard what happened," she said as she squeezed. "I'm so glad everyone's okay."

Before Amanda could recover from Melanie's onslaught, his sister was hugging him.

"And you! My God, I can't believe you charged right in there like John Wayne. Good thinking, taking one of the hunting horses who wouldn't freak over the gunshot."

Robbie couldn't guess how she'd heard about his

selection of the right mount in those nerve-racking seconds before he tore off after Kiefer, but Melanie had enough of their mother in her that she seemed to know what went on at Quest whether she was present or not.

Jenna called for the food to be brought out while insisting Melanie take a seat, but his sister didn't park herself for long. She stood in front of her plate with a glass of red wine in hand.

"I'd like to propose a toast." Her gaze swept the table, landing on Robbie, and in that moment he knew the news from the track was good.

And damned if his sister wasn't going to tout his victory in front of the whole family.

"To Robbie Preston, the best trainer around to have spotted the potential in a colt born too late in the year to be any good in most people's minds." She raised the glass higher. "Your colt set a new track record at the race today. Looks like Quest has found its next champion once the ban is lifted."

Robbie heard the collective intake of surprise all around the table. Beside him, Amanda squeezed his hand.

Then all at once, glasses lifted and slow smiles broke out. His mother cheered although his dad remained quiet. Kiefer didn't hold back however. The kid was out of his seat and pounding Robbie on the back while Max bounced around behind him.

His brothers drained their wineglasses and high-fived each other before congratulating him.

Robbie looked around the table and for the first

time in a long while he wondered if he could still make a place for himself here. But then, staying at Quest now was the coward's way out since he'd really be doing it because he wanted to be near Amanda. If he truly wanted the next move to be hers, he couldn't change the playing field so that she didn't have to make a move at all. He'd never know where he really stood with her.

At the head of the long dining table, Thomas cleared his throat.

"After one hell of a troubled summer, this is the best news our family has had in a long time." His eyes roved around the table as the server brought in trays of roast beef and potatoes, carrots and enough vats of gravy to feed the family, the staff and everyone in the neighborhood. "I know we've hired a head trainer recently—"

"We don't need to get into—" Robbie started, unwilling for Amanda to get drawn into the family debate.

"We do need to," Thomas contradicted. "I won't go so far as to say I made a mistake because I think Marcus Vasquez has a lot to offer any Thoroughbred operation."

O-kay.

And since when would Robbie expect his father to say he made a mistake anyhow? No news there. He felt Amanda shift closer to him in her chair, a silent show of support he appreciated even if he resented his father's need to go over old business now.

"Dad—" Melanie began, but their father waved away her comments too and continued to look at Robbie.

"I *will* say we're all the stronger for having both you and Marcus on board and I'd be damn sorry to lose you to a competitor, son."

All eyes turned to Robbie. Clearly the old man had heard about his interview in Texas. Still, his father didn't appear angry. Just serious. Unbending. But Robbie thought he saw respect in Thomas's eyes too.

Was that new or had it always been there and Robbie had missed seeing it because he'd been so preoccupied with the fact he wasn't a carbon copy of his brothers?

But maybe he wouldn't have been able to see it before knowing Amanda. Watching her with Kiefer and Max had given him a new appreciation for the way parents could love and respect each of their children, no matter how different they were. Maybe his parents had always understood him better than he thought; they'd simply been trying to guide his unruly butt in a productive direction all these years.

Robbie felt a new sense of belonging in the family—a family he now realized would only be complete when it included Amanda and her boys. The woman sitting next to him meant more to him than his father's approval and even more than his horses. Without her, none of it mattered.

Which made him wonder why the hell he was wolfing down roast beef without tasting it when what he really wanted was to plead his case better to Amanda. She'd told him she didn't want to follow him to Texas just for the sake of distancing herself from Orway, but damn it, he wanted her with him for more reasons than that and he understood that now.

"Will you excuse us for a minute?" Robbie rose from the table and placed his hand on Amanda's shoulder.

His father and brothers frowned in unison, matching expressions Robbie was no stranger to.

Amanda eased up from her chair, graceful and polite as she flashed her sweet smile around the table.

"We'll be right back." Laying her napkin on her chair, she followed him out of the dining room and into the conservatory, where one of the maids was arranging a vase of flowers. Plucking up her vase, she walked out of the room, discreetly leaving them alone.

Robbie's eyes went to Amanda and he knew his future rode on finding the right words now since he didn't want to put her in a position where she felt she couldn't say no. He would not take advantage of this woman's gratitude today of all days.

And, ah hell, he probably shouldn't even bring this up right now—

"I love you." Amanda's words knocked him on his butt faster than a rogue stallion on the first day of training.

He peeled himself off the floor in a figurative way and prayed he had heard what he thought he had heard.

"What?" His heart knocked louder against his chest, his whole body tensed for her answer, the clarification he'd give anything to hear.

A tiny furrow formed between her pretty eyes.

"I said, well, maybe it's a bit soon to feel this way, but I love—"

Robbie snatched her up in his arms so fast she didn't get to finish the sentence. Her mouth was muffled against his shirt, but he couldn't seem to loosen his hold on this wise and wonderful woman who had such a sweet impulsiveness in her nature no matter how reserved she tried to play it. In that instant, he was already planning when he would ask her to marry him.

Amanda pushed against Robbie's hold just a little until she realized he wasn't letting her go anytime soon. And that was just fine with her. She could have remained there, her head tipped against his chest, her cheek grazing the fabric of the crisp blue dress shirt he'd changed into for dinner.

When he finally eased away slightly, he let his hands roam over her back, dipping treacherously low before skimming all the way up to her shoulders again.

"It's not too soon to feel that way when you're strong and confident and know what you want in life." He tipped her chin with one hand and his blue eyes met hers. "And I can say that with all kinds of authority because I realized today that I love you too, Amanda Emory. Too much to let go of what we have just because I was too scared to wade in deeper and too afraid I'd hurt you somehow."

"You wouldn't." She threaded her fingers through two of the belt loops at the back of his pants.

"I wouldn't mean to, but I saw what Brent went

through after he lost his wife so I have an idea how much you've been through. I'd never want to add to that."

"Are you crazy? You're going to make me happier than I've ever been as soon as you tell me where I can sign on for our Texas relocation so we can be together."

She felt firm in her decision. Home wasn't here, no matter how much she liked Quest. Home was with Robbie, wherever he might go.

"Seriously?" His eyes lit with a fire and a joy she had never seen before and she experienced a surge of pure pleasure at being the woman to have put it there.

"We go where you go. Assuming you're willing to buy into the package deal that is my family." She knew Robbie was great with kids and he knew she cared about them or he wouldn't have looked so shaken today over what had happened to Kiefer.

But what she was asking him for was no small commitment. She wanted to be sure Robbie understood that by getting involved with them he had the power to break more hearts than just hers.

"I bought into it weeks ago at the U of L game. I had more fun hanging out with you and the kids than—shoot. I don't think I've ever felt so much a part of a family as I did that day."

"I'm so glad." Amanda's heart hurt for the problems Robbie had had with the Preston clan, but she loved hearing that he felt at home with them. With her.

"But I don't know about Texas—"

Her heart took a nosedive, and before he could explain, a soft knock sounded at the door.

"We're in here," Robbie called, clearly hoping the visitor would go away.

"Robbie, I think you'll want to hear about this." His father's voice was pitched low as he spoke just outside the door.

After exchanging a confused glance with Robbie, Amanda shrugged and nodded for him to let his father in.

"Come in." Robbie turned toward his dad, keeping an arm looped around Amanda's waist. "Sorry to miss so much of dinner, but we have a lot of things to discuss."

Thomas nodded, his keen blue eyes taking in both of them.

"I realize that and I'm sorry to intrude, but I thought this might have some bearing on whatever the two of you need to—work out." Clearing his throat, he walked around an overstuffed loveseat and dug a bottle of bourbon out of a sleek maple liquor cabinet. "I didn't want to make a big announcement in front of the family, but I thought I'd approach you discreetly to offer you the job I should have offered you earlier this year. You've got damn fine instincts when it comes to horses. I should have trusted in that sooner."

Not even glancing Robbie's way, he poured three glasses about two fingers full.

Amanda peered up at Robbie, the man she'd fallen

in love with, the man who'd been denied acceptance here for so long. His jaw was dragging close to the floor.

"What about Marcus?"

Thomas shrugged. "I'd speak to Marcus privately. I think we could offer him a good enough settlement to smooth over any hard feelings."

He handed Robbie and her each a glass.

Amanda waited to raise hers in a toast to the dream job Robbie had always wanted.

"No." Robbie shook his head, his refusal firm. "I wouldn't want to undermine him when he hasn't done anything wrong here. As you said, the operation will benefit from his guidance as long as he wants to stay."

Amanda hoped his father would argue the point, but instead he just nodded. Resolute. Uncompromising.

"Does that mean you're leaving us?"

"I was just discussing it with Amanda. I don't think I would leave after all, at least not now, knowing I'd have a shot at the top slot whenever Marcus decides to go. And maybe it wouldn't hurt to spend time with a trainer whose work is so respected even if his methods are a lot different than mine." He winked at Amanda. "It'll keep me humble for a little while longer."

"Fair enough." Downing his bourbon, Thomas set the glass on the tray and patted Amanda awkwardly on the back, even though he didn't offer any sign of affection for his son. Perhaps his warmth toward her was his way of being kind to Robbie.

"I'm glad to hear you're staying since I'd hate to lose my son *and* the new office manager." He managed a smile for Amanda. "My wife says you're doing a bang-up job and she'll tell you all about her new incentive plan for employees who are interested in obtaining their degree. Not that you'd need it to stay on here, but it's a good way to pay the bill if you're considering it."

The bonus was such an unexpected surprise even in an evening full of unexpected things. Amanda had always regretted dropping out.

"Thank you, Mr. Preston." Unwilling to settle for the cool distance on a day so full of emotions, Amanda gave him a quick hug. "And thank you for being there for me today with all the help to search for Kiefer."

He hugged her back. Just a brief squeeze of his arms, but it was there.

"You're welcome. And I hope you make it back to the table in time for dessert. The cook's baked Alaska is sort of an event around here."

Watching him leave and close the doors behind him, Amanda wheeled around to Robbie.

"That's the job you wanted!" She knew how badly he longed for that recognition. Why hadn't he jumped at the chance?

"And I have the feeling it will be mine one of these days, but maybe what I wanted more than anything was the recognition of my capabilities." He drained his bourbon and then set their glasses aside. "And I'd say I got that. Along with much, much more."

His nostrils flared as he leaned closer, his arms wrapping around her waist.

"So you're going to cancel the interview?" Her heart thudded in her chest, her hopes for the future swelling bigger with each passing moment.

"Yes ma'am, I am. I think I'll stick it out here after all. That is, unless you have a sudden hankering for west Texas."

Her whole body warmed in response to his, her skin tingling at his touch.

"No. But I have a sudden hankering for something else." She nipped at his jaw, arching up on her toes to slide her body meaningfully over his.

"I'm guessing it's not baked Alaska?"

"It's something even sweeter."

"Do you know we've got a room full of family to face now?" He groaned as he planted a kiss on her neck.

"Yes, but just keep thinking about the fact that there's a sleepover here tonight." She tilted her head to one side to give him better access and his mouth brushed wicked kisses down her throat into the neckline of her dress. "You can show me your skills at sneaking around in your parents' house without anyone hearing."

"Leave your door unlocked," he warned. "I'm going to remind you all night long why being together is such a damn good idea."

"I hope you're discreet, Robbie Preston, or it won't be just that horse of yours giving everyone something to talk about."

* * * * *

*Ladies, start your engines with a sneak preview
of Harlequin's officially licensed
NASCAR® romance series.*

Life in a famous racing family comes at a price

All his life Larry Grosso has lived in the shadow
of his well-known racing family—but it's now
time for him to take what he wants. And on top
of that list is Crystal Hayes—breathtaking,
sweet…and twenty-two years younger. But
their age difference is creating animosity within
their families, and suddenly their romance is
the talk of the entire NASCAR circuit!

*Turn the page for a sneak preview of
OVERHEATED
by Barbara Dunlop
On sale July 29 wherever books are sold.*

RUFUS, as Crystal Hayes had decided to call the black Lab, slept soundly on the soft seat even as she maneuvered the Softco truck in front of the Dean Grosso garage. Engines fired through the open bay doors, compressors clacked and impact tools whined as the teams tweaked their race cars in preparation for qualifying at the third race in Charlotte.

As always when she visited the garage area, Crystal experienced a vicarious thrill, watching the technicians' meticulous, last-minute preparations. As the daughter of a machinist, she understood the difference a fraction of a degree or a thousandth of an inch could make in the performance of a race car.

She muscled the driver's door shut behind her and waved hello to a couple of familiar crew members in their white-and-pale-blue jump suits. Then she rounded the back of the truck and rolled up the door. Inside, five boxes were marked Cargill Motors.

One of them was big and heavy, and it had slid forward a few feet, probably when she'd braked to make the narrow parking lot entrance. So she pushed up the sleeves of her canary-yellow T-shirt, then stretched forward to reach the box. A couple of catcalls came her way as her faded blue jeans tightened across her rear end. But she knew they were good-natured, and she simply ignored them.

She dragged the box toward her over the gritty metal floor.

"Let me give you a hand with that," a deep, melodious voice rumbled in her ear.

"I can manage," she responded crisply, not wanting to engage with any of the catcallers.

Here in the garage, the last thing she needed was one of the guys treating her as if she was something other than, well, one of the guys.

She'd learned long ago there was something about her that made men toss out pickup lines like parade candy. And she'd been around race crews long enough to know she needed to behave like a buddy, not a potential date.

She piled the smaller boxes on top of the large one.

"It looks heavy," said the voice.

"I'm tough," she assured him as she scooped the pile into her arms.

He didn't move away, so she turned her head to subject him to a *back off* stare. But she found herself staring into a compelling pair of green...no, brown...no, hazel eyes. She did a double take as they seemed to twinkle, multicolored, under the garage lights.

The man insistently held out his hands for the

boxes. There was a dignity in his tone and little crinkles around his eyes that hinted at wisdom. There wasn't a single sign of flirtation in his expression, but Crystal was still cautious.

"You know I'm being paid to move this, right?" she asked him.

"That doesn't mean I can't be a gentleman."

Somebody whistled from a workbench. "Go, Professor Larry."

The man named Larry tossed a "Back off" over his shoulder. Then he turned to Crystal. "Sorry about that."

"Are you for real?" she asked, growing uncomfortable with the attention they were drawing. The last thing she needed was some latter-day Sir Galahad defending her honor at the track.

He quirked a dark eyebrow in a question.

"I mean," she elaborated, "you don't need to worry. I've been fending off the wolves since I was seventeen."

"Doesn't make it right," he countered, attempting to lift the boxes from her hands.

She jerked back. "You're not making it any easier."

He frowned.

"You carry this box, and they start thinking of me as a girl."

Professor Larry dipped his gaze to take in the curves of her figure. "Hate to tell you this," he said, a little twinkle coming into those multifaceted eyes.

Something about his look made her shiver inside. It was a ridiculous reaction. Guys had given her the once-over a million times. She'd learned long ago to ignore it.

"Odds are," Larry continued, a teasing drawl in his tone, "they already have."

She turned pointedly away, boxes in hand as she marched across the floor. She could feel him watching her from behind.

* * * * *

Crystal Hayes could do without her looks,
men obsessed with her looks, and guys who
think they're God's gift to the ladies.
Would Larry be the one guy who could blow all
of Crystal's preconceptions away?
Look for OVERHEATED
by Barbara Dunlop.
On sale July 29, 2008.

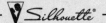

Harlequin® Historical
Historical Romantic Adventure!

From *USA TODAY*
bestselling author
Margaret Moore

A LOVER'S KISS

A Frenchwoman in London,
Juliette Bergerine is unexpectedly
thrown together in hiding with
Sir Douglas Drury. As lust and
desire give way to deeper emotions,
how will Juliette react on discovering
that her brother was murdered—
by Drury!

*Available September
wherever you buy books.*

REQUEST YOUR FREE BOOKS!

2 FREE NOVELS PLUS 2 FREE GIFTS!

Silhouette®

SPECIAL EDITION®

Life, Love and Family!

YES! Please send me 2 FREE Silhouette Special Edition® novels and my 2 FREE gifts (gifts are worth about $10). After receiving them, if I don't wish to receive any more books, I can return the shipping statement marked "cancel." If I don't cancel, I will receive 6 brand-new novels every month and be billed just $4.24 per book in the U.S. or $4.99 per book in Canada, plus 25¢ shipping and handling per book and applicable taxes, if any*. That's a savings of at least 15% off the cover price! I understand that accepting the 2 free books and gifts places me under no obligation to buy anything. I can always return a shipment and cancel at any time. Even if I never buy another book from Silhouette, the two free books and gifts are mine to keep forever.

235 SDN EEYU 335 SDN EEY6

Name	(PLEASE PRINT)	
Address		Apt. #
City	State/Prov.	Zip/Postal Code

Signature (if under 18, a parent or guardian must sign)

Mail to the **Silhouette Reader Service:**
IN U.S.A.: P.O. Box 1867, Buffalo, NY 14240-1867
IN CANADA: P.O. Box 609, Fort Erie, Ontario L2A 5X3

Not valid to current subscribers of Silhouette Special Edition books.

Want to try two free books from another line?
Call 1-800-873-8635 or visit www.morefreebooks.com.

* Terms and prices subject to change without notice. N.Y. residents add applicable sales tax. Canadian residents will be charged applicable provincial taxes and GST. Offer not valid in Quebec. This offer is limited to one order per household. All orders subject to approval. Credit or debit balances in a customer's account(s) may be offset by any other outstanding balance owed by or to the customer. Please allow 4 to 6 weeks for delivery. Offer available while quantities last.

Your Privacy: Silhouette is committed to protecting your privacy. Our Privacy Policy is available online at www.eHarlequin.com or upon request from the Reader Service. From time to time we make our lists of customers available to reputable third parties who may have a product or service of interest to you. If you would prefer we not share your name and address, please check here. ☐

SSE08R

Inside ROMANCE

Stay up-to-date on all your
romance reading news!

Inside Romance is a FREE quarterly newsletter
highlighting our upcoming series releases
and promotions.

Visit
www.eHarlequin.com/InsideRomance
to sign up to receive our complimentary newsletter today!

IRN11107

▼ *Silhouette*®

SPECIAL EDITION™

NEW YORK TIMES BESTSELLING AUTHOR

DIANA PALMER

A brand-new Long, Tall Texans novel

HEART OF STONE

Feeling unwanted and unloved, Keely returns to Jacobsville and to Boone Sinclair, a rancher troubled by his own past. Boone has always seemed reserved, but now Keely discovers a sensuality with him that quickly turns to love. Can they each see past their own scars to let love in?

Available September 2008 wherever you buy books.